Barcelona Tales

Barcelona Tales

Stories translated by

Peter Bush

Edited by

Helen Constantine

OXFORD
UNIVERSITY PRESS

OXFORD
UNIVERSITY PRESS

Great Clarendon Street, Oxford, OX2 6DP,
United Kingdom

Oxford University Press is a department of the University of Oxford.
It furthers the University's objective of excellence in research, scholarship,
and education by publishing worldwide. Oxford is a registered trade mark of
Oxford University Press in the UK and in certain other countries

First Edition published in 2019

Impression: 1

Published in the United States of America by Oxford University Press
198 Madison Avenue, New York, NY 10016, United States of America

British Library Cataloguing in Publication Data
Data available

Library of Congress Control Number: 2018965640

ISBN 978–0–19–879837–8

Printed and bound in Great Britain by
Clays Ltd, Elcograf S.p.A.

Contents

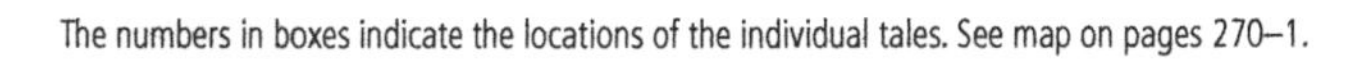

The numbers in boxes indicate the locations of the individual tales. See map on pages 270–1.

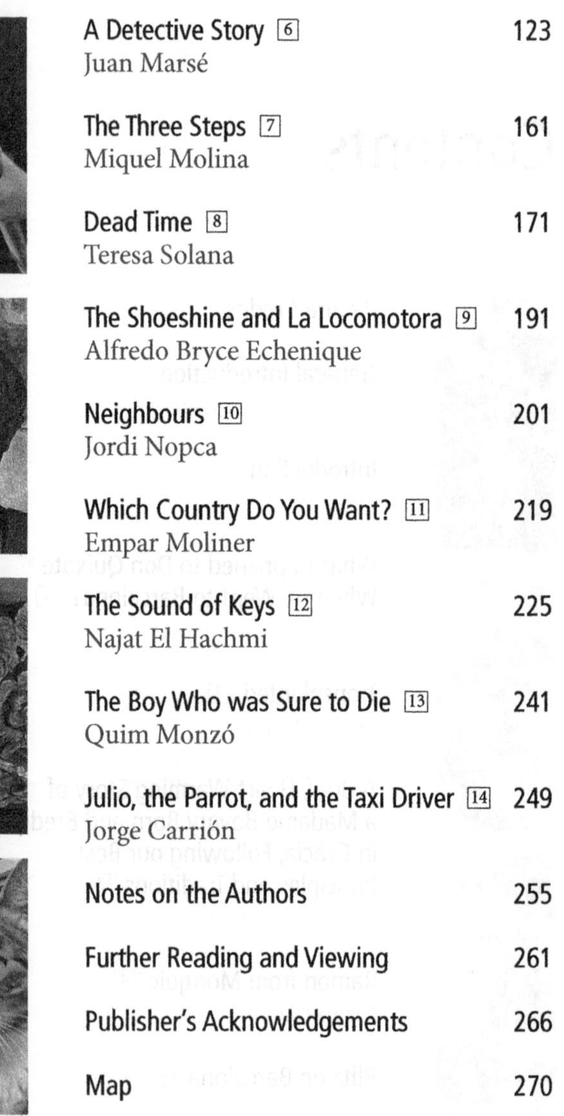

Picture Credits

Page 22: engraving by Gustave Doré. Dover Publications

Page 46: Prisma Archivo/Alamy Stock Photo

Page 76: Interfoto/Alamy Stock Photo

Page 102: foottoo © 123RF.com

Page 112: Photo 12/Alamy Stock Photo

Page 122: Heritage Image Partnership Ltd/Alamy Stock Photo

Page 160: natursports © 123RF

Page 170: Universal Images Group North America LLC/Alamy Stock Photo

Page 190: © Daniel Farson/Stringer/Getty Images

Page 200: Peter Forsberg/Alamy Stock Photo

Page 218: Pixabay

Page 224: Stefano Politi Markovina/Alamy Stock Photo

Page 240: © Spencer Means (CC BY-SA 2.0)

Page 248: © Jorge Carrión

Page 270: map produced by Phoenix Mapping © Oxford University Press

General Introduction

Arriving in Barcelona is always an adventure, albeit on occasions rather too exciting. Miguel de Cervantes, in 1575 travelling to Spain from Naples, was attacked by pirates as he approached Barcelona and taken captive. He drew on these dramatic experiences in the 'Captive's Tale' in *Don Quixote*, the first tale translated in this anthology. In another story, titled 'Transplanted', Friar Baker, admittedly no Don Quixote, but a baker by trade, is very excited on arrival in the capital from his small village in rural Catalonia to visit his son, who has hit the big time by opening a hairdresser's salon in the city:

Words can't describe the baker's impressions as he crosses La Rambla. The coloured lights of carriages moving in different directions, the people seated in trams, the flood of light from shops, the huddles of window-shoppers, the crowd strolling under the trees, the bright publicity hoardings; everything seems strange in his eyes and makes him dizzy.

He thinks Barcelona is heaven because of the lights and hell because of the din.

In the story 'Neighbours', Jia has come all the way from China, to open a bar. This vibrant city is also a magnet for the two girls in 'The Sound of Keys' who move, like the baker, from their home in the provinces to a flat in the centre of the capital.

Barcelona in the twenty-first century continues to attract, as it always has, the traveller, and not just because of its football team. It is a thriving, wealthy city, with a mass of things to entertain its many tourists: the beaches at Barceloneta, the port, the Gaudí architecture, the medieval centre, the shopping, and the many markets—the Ninot market, recently refurbished and the setting for Teresa Solana's story, is just one of about forty in the city. In *Homage to Catalonia* George Orwell wrote of his arrival there in 1936:

> Down the Ramblas . . . the loudspeakers were bellowing revolutionary songs all day and far into the night. . . . In outward appearance it was a town in which the wealthy classes had practically ceased to exist.

He could never have imagined that it would become such an attractive and popular destination, rivalling Paris and Venice in its lure for the modern tourist.

Not long after Orwell's time in the city, where he had arrived hoping to work as a journalist but straight away joined the militia and espoused the internationalist cause, came the terrible bombing by Italian fascist planes in 1938. The destruction of the city and its inhabitants are poignantly evoked in the story by Jordana, 'Blitz on Barcelona'. Subsequently and for much of the twentieth century, the Catalans, like the rest of Spain, suffered under the military dictatorship of Franco, only emerging from this on his death in 1975. Understandable, therefore, after the suppression of the Catalan language among other things, that there has grown up a spirit of resistance in this fiercely independent country, proud of its traditions and achievements.

Whether you go to Barcelona to admire the modernist architecture of Antoni Gaudi's houses and churches, or for the fun of the many street parties in the *barrios* and the almost non-stop festivals and celebrations, these stories of Catalonia, translated by a long-time resident, and conveying, as they do, the extraordinary vitality and variety of this most international of capital cities, will be certain to please and excite.

Helen Constantine

Introduction

Long before I started learning Spanish or even knew of the existence of the Catalan language, I had heard of Barcelona, or rather the fall of Barcelona and the Second Republic, the triumphal entry of Franco and his troops into the city, and the thousands of refugees streaming along tracks and roads to the French border on their way to exile. My father had seen the newsreel images and photos in the newspapers and it spurred him on to join the British Army as a volunteer 'to stop fascism taking over Europe' and it would be his preface to our occasional 'what Dad did in the war' conversations.

By the time I first visited the city in 1968, I had read George Orwell's account of the civil war in *Homage to Catalonia*, and studied medieval and modern Spanish history. I knew that Barcelona had been an important Roman port and then capital of a kingdom where five languages flourished—Arabic, Castilian, Catalan, French, and Hebrew—and whose empire reached as far as Rhodes and imposed its maritime law throughout the Mediterranean.

I knew that the year-long siege of Barcelona in 1714 signalled the end of the last vestiges of independence and Catalonia's incorporation into the Spanish nation-state that now presided over the now-moribund empire initiated by Ferdinand and Isabel in 1492 with the expulsion of the Jews, the expansion of the Inquisition, and the conquest of most of Latin America. However, Spain's Industrial Revolution began in Catalonia and its capital was soon being hailed as the 'Manchester' of the Iberian Peninsula. If the Catalan language was reduced to being a domestic vernacular in the eighteenth century, Barcelona and the Catalan-speaking areas extending to south of Alicante and including the Balearic Islands and Alghero in Sardinia began a renaissance that established Barcelona and these areas as the bilingual communities they are today, despite the thirty-six years of General Franco's dictatorship that once again banned the language from general public use.

After the Olympic Games and the celebrations around the 'discovery' of the Americas in 1992 established the brand of Barcelona as an international, cosmopolitan city with its painters—Picasso and Miró—its modernist architecture—Gaudí—and later its style of football—Johan Cruyff, Messi, and Pep Guardiola—it has become one of the most visited cities in Europe with huge cruise ships lining up to enter its harbour and hen and stag parties from all over Europe romping in the bars and on the beaches of the Barceloneta and the Port Olímpic. Town Hall politicians, whether socialist or conservative, have cultivated the city's arty, trendy, and mass-market appeal to the point that locals can't afford to rent or buy, find their spaces for entertainment overpriced, and now demonstrate against the tourist invasion.

In 1968 it wasn't like that. The city was shabby; grey and black were the predominant colours. Gaudí's masterpiece, La Pedrera, on the Paseo de Gracia (as it was known then) was a sombre grey; his Parc Güell was overgrown, strewn with litter, almost abandoned; and the unfinished spires of the Sagrada Familia soot-black. I was in the city for six weeks researching the origins of the workers' movement after the 1868 Revolution and stayed in a boarding house that was mainly for permanent residents: single men who sat singly at tables to eat breakfast, lunch, and evening meal and I did likewise and never spoke to a soul. I walked daily through the red-light district of the *barrio chino* behind La Rambla (now the thriving El Raval with a mainly Muslim population) to the library in the old medieval hospital buildings (now the National Library of Catalonia) and then to the Correos on the seafront to collect my mail from the *poste restante*. Groups of skinny men stood threateningly on street corners; fat women in garish skirts wearing bright red lipstick sat in bar windows or outside doors to brothels; the menacing *guardia civil* patrolled; the feared Police Headquarters where oppositionists were jailed and tortured on Via Layetana was a few minutes away; all newspapers were in Spanish and only reported on Spain's successes and the latest acts of Generalísimo Franco. Barcelona wasn't an immediately friendly city; it seemed more like a city under occupation.

Fifty years later, there are two Catalan daily newspapers, several online, and two that publish in Spanish and Catalan, several Catalan TV channels, Wikipedia in Catalan, and the vehicle of education is Catalan: most people are at least bilingual. Millions have demonstrated festively through the streets of Barcelona for the right to preserve the status of Catalan and the right to have a referendum to vote for independence and for the release of political leaders who are in prison and the return of those in exile.

As the stories in this anthology show, Barcelona has also been a city that has had migrants and other visitors for different reasons at different stages in its development and like most great ports, it is forced to look outwards. And as a port, with an industrial hinterland, it has also a tradition of class conflict and strikes. Social class plays an important role in the composition of the districts that make up the city in general lines from proletarian El Carmelo and the Guinardó to patrician Pedralbes and Sarrià on southern and northern heights, respectively. The upper and professional middle classes favour the blocks of flats on the grid system of streets of the Eixample designed by Ildefonso Cerdà in the late nineteenth-century to cope with the influx of moneyed families from old colonies like Cuba as a result of independence movements and of landowners from rural Catalonia in flight from the banditry and lawlessness that was the legacy of the third Carlist war. The city has been and is a melting pot in a series of 'villages' that retain their character or adapt according to the weight of demographic change, and rarely without major political events looming. It is hardly surprising that Barcelona has inspired writers from Miguel de Cervantes onwards and that they have been inventive in their ways of telling.

When Don Quixote and Sancho Panza arrive in Barcelona, they do so as celebrities. The first part of Cervantes's novel was published in 1605 and soon became a bestseller for its day and many citizens have heard of them in the second part of the novel published in 1615. It is St John's Eve, which is still one of the city's major festivals with music, dancing, and fireworks. The reader has the sense of a walled city that is vibrant and wealthy though bandits abound in the countryside and pirates in the Mediterranean. From rural La Mancha it is the eccentric pair's first sight of the sea, of galley slaves, and of a publisher's premises. Sancho is shocked by the nakedness of the slaves and the way they are whipped. Don Quixote is flattered by the attention he receives but annoyed that some of this may be down to a spurious Second Part written by a fan of Lope de Vega, and storms out of the printshop when he sees they have that false sequel on their presses. As the galley they board pursues a pirate ship, the Barcelona sequence develops into what seems a tale of romance and disguises, but 1615 was only a few years after the expulsion of the *moriscos*, the Muslims who stayed on after decrees earlier in the previous century had expelled them for not converting to Christianity. Over half a million stayed and converted while continuing to practice their Muslim religion in private. The 1609 decree of expulsion was the final warning and most departed to North Africa, though many subsequently returned. The conversations and decisions on behalf of the *moriscos* and Turkish sailors threatened with being strung up from the ship's mast reflect then the tolerance of Cervantes and the tolerance that existed in Barcelona despite the power of the Inquisition.

One of Cervantes's favourite novels was the chivalresque *Tirant lo Blanc*, written in Catalan and published at the end of the fifteenth century. The Catalan tradition of writing fiction was only properly resumed in the second half of the nineteenth century after a literary renaissance inspired by a desire to resurrect the written language prepared the way for the realist novels and stories of Narcís Oller and others. In the story 'Transplanted' Oller reflects ironically on the optimistic belief in Progress espoused by Barcelona's nouveau riche middle classes and, particularly on the attraction of the city's lights to a retired baker and his hairdresser son from a remote village. Dazzled by the glitter, Daniel, 'Friar Baker', abandons his comfortable routines of a lifetime in a place where he is known and respected for the excitement of the La Rambla and the borrowed glory of his son's entrepreneurial success, funded by the money he had made as a diligent baker. In the end, like many a migrant to the big city, he finds only solitude among the crowds: the romance of trains, trams, and gas-lights is short-lived, his son is too busy making it, and he retreats to the rail station hoping to bump into someone from his village, his gaze gliding along the rails 'like the gaze of an exile contemplating a river that finds its source in his distant land'.

Gràcia is a district of high, narrow streets and leafy squares that every summer is home to a fiesta when streets are colourfully decorated by committees of neighbours and dancing and carousing goes on deep into the night. It is also renowned for its clothes designers, furniture makers, and artisan traditions, and a long-standing resident Roma community. Small workshops abound as do bars and restaurants. The local politics are usually thought of as being radical and republican and can extend from New Age life-styles to anarchist squatters. However, Montserrat Roig's story reminds us that the district had and has its more well-heeled inhabitants, traditionally connected to the textile industry that was so key in the Catalan economy. The diary-cum-letter of her narrator follows her life from late adolescence to a marriage of convenience to a boring, but rich, businessman that helps her father's firm. The story spans the period from 7 November 1883 when she came out in society at the Liceu Opera and an anarchist threw a bomb, to the loss of Cuba, one of Spain's last colonies in 1898, and a place where many Catalans became wealthy whether from sugar plantation and slave ownership or distilling rum like the Bacardí family, to the Setmana Trágica in May 1909 when troops fought and killed striking workers. It is the portrait of a rich young woman trapped in a marriage and set of customs she dislikes and describes in ironic detail, but that she can't relinquish. She painfully details her grandmother's death, funeral, and the family pantheon in the Les Corts cemetery as redolent of the pursuit of pompous appearance, in a futile attempt to defeat transience and ensure the survival of the dynasty through granite and marble. She herself has no sense of progress, only of deadening tradition that is alleviated by the purchase of the latest fashions from Paris or slap-up dinners in Barcelona's French-style restaurants. Hers is a claustrophobic existence that seems blind to the rest of Gràcia and prefers to ignore the passage of history. She knows—remotely—that there is another world out there, but can't flee her cosseted surroundings or the husband who pursues her with his banal love poems.

Josep Pla couldn't wait for Sunday to come when he was released from the tedious round of law lectures and rote-learning at the University of Barcelona and could explore the rest of the city. From a small hamlet near Palafrugell on the Costa Brava, Pla loved the city as a flaneur and enjoyed striking up conversations and friendships with all and sundry. His story 'Ramon from Montjuic' was published in 1925 and refers to his student days in 1919. He loved to climb up the hill–now the site for the Joan Miró museum–and survey the city and gaze at 'the wintry Barcelona sky, which is beautiful, especially on windy days—a sky where white clumps of clouds scudded over warm blues, faded greens and crimson haze'. His description of his bohemian friend Ramon's one-man fairground and dance hall and the taverns and streets of working-class Poble-sec where migrants from Aragon and Castile, sailors, and the war-wounded try to find cheap entertainment shows there was plenty of life away from La Rambla. The story was published during the dictatorship of Primo de Rivera when Pla was briefly exiled for his opposition to the colonial war being fought by the dictator in Morocco where thousands of Spanish troops and Moroccan independence fighters were slaughtered and a young soldier by the name of Francisco Franco was showing his brutal form.

Which brings us to C. A. Jordana's 'Blitz on Barcelona'. Barcelona was subjected to heavy bombing by Italian planes from their base in Majorca throughout 1938. Like the German bombing of Guernika in the Basque country, the raids were indiscriminate and aimed at the civilian population as well as shopping and other civilian areas rather than military targets. By that time, the city was no longer the optimistic hive of anarchist revolution where all was collectivized and the International Brigades thronged the streets. It was a city under siege where food was in short supply. Jordana was a Catalan writer and translator who belonged to a group of socialist artists and intellectuals who campaigned on behalf of the beleaguered Republic. These vignettes were published at the time in the weekly magazine *Meridià*. They are remarkable in that Jordana uses modernist techniques he picked up from translating Virginia Woolf and D. H. Lawrence and not the usual realist approach to writing about the war. His bitter irony and lyrical immediacy communicate the fear and resilience of ordinary citizens as they try to lead their lives while awaiting the next raid, or help those who have already been wounded. Jordana went to Chile and Argentina and never returned from exile to live in Spain.

Juan Marsé's 'A Detective Story' is located in the post-war period in the Carmelo district on the city's southern heights where migrants from the south—Andalusia, Murcia, and Almeria–flocked to escape dire rural poverty. The narrator and his trio of teenage friends sit in a clapped-out 1941 Lincoln Continental on a Saturday afternoon in 'an April that seemed more like November' and play at being detectives, imagining they are in one of their favourite Hollywood films trailing a young woman. As the boss of the gang is one Juanito Marés—a play on the author's name—the story draws in part on Marsé's memories of growing up in those grey times when Franco's fascist party, the Falange, ruled the roost and extortion, betrayal, and torture were the order of the day in El Carmelo and carob jam was a luxury. The young lads' exciting, sometimes lurid, fantasies, powered by films like Jules Dassin's 1948 *The Naked City* or Sax Rohmer's novels, are their way of coping with the seediness of the adult world where Marés's mother and her bohemian friends drink and sing music-hall songs to drown their sorrows, Roca, the narrator's father, is in prison for being a 'red and a separatist', and the city they gaze down at 'squats in the distance, like a silted pond, like stagnant water'.

When Miquel Molina's narrator in 'The Three Steps' returns to visit those steps and heights, inspired by a re-reading of a novel one assumes to be by Marsé, it is a different Barcelona and he is a middle-class youth who has had other options. The path is crowded by tourists and runners. He has just spent five years studying as a postgraduate in foreign universities. The civil war and Francoist Spain are the stuff of fiction and the streets now have Catalan names. When he decides to walk down from the Bare Mountain to the city centre—'This mountain to sea route... a delightfully Barcelonan thing', he passes endless blocks of flats and where there was once the odd bar, there are now many and restaurants offering 'exotic' food. (Nothing can rival a stroll from the top of Barcelona to the sea on a sunny day!) He is going to celebrate one of the most festive days in the local calendar, the Day of the Book and the Rose, the Dia de Sant Jordi, April 23, when the streets are full of stalls selling books and roses, which sell in their thousands. He joins a queue waiting for his author to sign his copy of the novel.

Every district in Barcelona has its market and many are fine late-nineteenth-century *modernista* wrought-iron buildings. *Barceloneses* still prefer to shop at real butchers, fishmongers, greengrocers, and fruiterers. Over the past decade many of the old markets have been refurbished, like the Mercat de la Libertat off Gran de Gràcia or El Ninot on Carrer Mallorca in Eixample, and they aren't so full of tourists as the Boquería on La Rambla. El Ninot as the location of Teresa Solana's noir tale of a serial killer points to the way that the stall owners have to resort to Carnival or Halloween decorations and disguises and other such attractions to keep their clientele and also to the way the bourgeois neighbourhood has transformed like the city itself into a place 'whose mestizo vocation and diversity of accents seems endless'. Her protagonists are female. One, Soledad, is a butcher who has come to live in Barcelona from the mainly working-class area of Santa Coloma and the other is the police inspector on the case, Aurora. Though a noir, the focus is not on the killer and his victims but the mind and emotions of Soledad, who is privately driven to investigate the case and the strategies the police inspector devises. Written in 2016, the tale, unlike Marsé's, has a female perspective, though it too has a twist, suggesting that the histories, memories, and lives of families are still tainted by the crimes of the dictatorship.

I once chatted to a butcher in a small bar by the Plaça Reial who had come to Barcelona from Pakistan. He told me of his long odyssey that included years working as a coal miner in León where he said the tunnels were particularly deep and dangerous. His friend, from Beirut, told me about the civil war in the Lebanon and the ignorance in Spain as regards the country's Arab heritage, the Alhambra, the kingdom of Granada,... He worked in a hotel. We walk the streets of cities like Barcelona, use the services, but the bustle conceals several kinds of solitude, faces that are mere faces in a crowd or behind a counter, and not merely for tourists: urban loneliness and anonymity is endemic. Some of the stories here attempt to break that static, surface interaction and enable the reader to imagine the emotions and experiences behind the polite masks. The Peruvian lover of literature in Alfredo Bryce Echenique's story fetches up as a receptionist on the night shift in a cheap hotel near the University of Barcelona, the ideal employment for an avid reader who also has a passion for shiny shoes. Eleodoro Holguín, who managed to fail three university degrees in Lima, has journeyed from one country to the next in Europe, to which he migrated with much loftier hopes.

Barcelona is a city surrounded by sea and mountains with little room for expansion, so most inhabitants live in flats. I lived in the city for ten years from 2003 and experienced the tensions that can exist in those blocks; one scary committee was chaired by a French Nazi who had escaped to a safe haven from democratic justice in 1945. The Chinese couple, imagined by Jordi Nopca, ran a bar next to the old Filmoteca (it has since moved to much grander premises in El Raval). They are hardworking and happy and feel they are lucky, but that's before they fall foul of the misfortunes of a customer with a penchant for gin and tonics whose neighbours seem to have sinister intentions.

Not far away, in San Gervasi, Empar Moliner reminds us that for all its radical and revolutionary reputation, Barcelona has a large number of churches, convents, and Catholics and that the lives of not just the wealthy are cushioned by a host of maids, domestic cleaners, and child and grandparent-minders, mainly from Latin America: the nuns in her Convent of the Immaculate Conception are the blustery or officious go-betweens matching women with families. At the other end of town, off the Avenida Mediterránea, where the massive new shopping, hotel, and restaurant complex of Les Glòries has been built and the old second market of Les Encants has been moved into new shiny premises, the two sisters in Najat El Hachmi's story seem to be enjoying a newly found freedom in their two-roomed flat on the Pasatge Vintró. They have left the rest of their migrant Moroccan family in a suburb of a dull provincial town, because they can no longer stand the strict discipline imposed by their traditional parents, or the daily chore of dealing with their brothers' dirty underpants. But, after the briefest 'honeymoon' period, they find they are pulled in opposite directions by the attractions of the big city. One works washing dishes in restaurant and the other cleaning rooms in a hotel. One likes bikinis, bars, and boys, and the other prefers the security of a community club run by 'our people'. Quim Monzó's story takes us into a grand flat in the Ensanche where a seamstress goes on a Thursday afternoon to sew and darn. She takes her son who is dazzled by the tidbits and drinks he is offered and by the games he can play with the son of the house. Nobody can imagine the expectations that might be generated by such an innocent friendship.

Finally, you can walk to most places in Barcelona, as there is an excellent public transport system. There are also taxis, and, if you are lucky, like Jorge Carrión, you may be blessed with a cab driver who doesn't want to talk about Real Madrid or Barça and he will tell you about his parrot.

You will find streets or characters with names spelled differently, depending on whether the writer is writing in Spanish or Catalan. *Bon viatge* or *buen viaje*!

Peter Bush

What Happened to Don Quixote When He Went to Barcelona?

Miguel de Cervantes

Don Quixote spent three nights and three days with Roque the bandit, though it felt like three centuries. He had plenty to look and wonder at in the way the bandits lived: they dawned in one place, ate in another; sometimes fleeing, not knowing who, at others waiting, not knowing for whom; they slept on their feet, woke up, and dashed everywhere. They dispatched spies, watched out for patrols, and rattled the few arquebus they possessed, because most used muskets. Roque spent nights far from his men, in spots unknown to them, because the many arrest warrants out on his life issued by the viceroy of Barcelona made him anxious and afraid; he dared trust nobody, and was afraid his own men might kill or hand him over to the enforcers of justice. It was a wretched, irksome life.

In the end, Roque, Don Quixote and Sancho Panza, and six other squires set out for Barcelona. They reached the city's beaches late in the night on St John's Eve, and Roque hugged Don Quixote and Sancho, handed them the ten escudos he had promised but not given them, and left, after offering every kind of help, which they graciously accepted.

After Roque's departure, Don Quixote stayed awake on his horse waiting for daybreak, and a pale-faced dawn soon peered over balconies to the east, cheering up herbs and flowers rather than his ears, though they were soon excited by the sound of fifes and drums and the jingle of bells, as well as what must have been hoodlums bawling 'Out of the way, out of the way' as they ran out of the city gates. Dawn yielded to the sun, and, larger than a buckler, its face gradually rose above the dip of the horizon.

Don Quixote and Sancho couldn't believe their eyes: they were seeing the sea for the first time, and it loomed broader and vaster than the Ruidera lagoons they knew from La Mancha: they saw galleys by the beach, their awnings being lowered to reveal pennants and streamers that fluttered in the wind, and kissed and caressed the water; from their decks bugles, fifes, and trumpets filled the air with both gentle and war-like sounds. The galleys swayed and skirmished on the placid water and were almost outdone by a huge number of gentlemen in bright livery who rode out of the city on handsome horses. The soldiers in the galleys fired their artillery and from city walls and towers heavy guns blasted the air, making a horrendous racket, and large cannon in the galleys' midships responded. The smiley sea, the festive land, and the bracing air, occasionally darkened by the smoke from artillery fire, seemed to raise everyone's spirits. Sancho couldn't fathom how those big hulks moving across the sea could have so many feet. That very second, the liveried gentlemen rode up, shouting, making a great bellicose hullaballoo, to an astonished, dumbstruck Don Quixote, and one of them, Roque's friend in Barcelona, proclaimed: 'Welcome to our city, mirror, lighthouse, star and magnet of all knight errantry, its finest representation; welcome, I say, valiant Don Quixote from La Mancha, and not that fake, fictitious, apocryphal fellow who recently appeared in deceitful stories, but the real, genuine, upstanding fellow described to us by the stellar historian, Cide Hamete Benengeli.'*

Don Quixote didn't utter a word, and nor did those gentlemen expect him to answer, but pressed by the crowds coming behind, they now pranced and wheeled around him, and he turned to Sancho and said: 'You see, these people know who we are: I bet they've read our story and even the one just published by that man from Aragon.'

* Alonso Fernández de Avellaneda's sequel to Cervantes's novel was published in 1614. Cervantes was furious. The narrator of Cervantes' novel always maintains that he picked up the manuscript in Toledo written in Arabized Spanish script and authored by the Arab historian Benengeli.

The gentleman who had addressed Don Quixote now added: 'Your very good sir, Don Quixote, come with us, for we are big friends of Roque Guinart and want to help you.'

To which Don Quixote replied: 'If courtesy breeds courtesy, then yours, good sir, is daughter or close relative to the great Roque's. Take me wherever you wish; whatever you want, I want too, and more so, if I can be of any service to you.'

The gentleman replied affably, and they escorted their visitors towards the city, to the sound of fifes and drums. When they passed through its gates, a bold, mischievous couple of lads, showing more devilry than the devil himself, left their gang of ragamuffins and penetrated the cortege. One lifted the tail of Sancho's donkey and the other, the tail of Don Quixote's steed, Rocinante, and stuck a bunch of gorse up their backsides. The poor beasts felt those spurs, and waved their tails, but the pain was excruciating and they reared a thousand times and threw their masters to the ground. An angry Don Quixote ran to remove the furze from his hack, and Sancho did likewise. Don Quixote's escorts tried in vain to punish the young ruffians: they had melted into the milling crowds.

Don Quixote and Sancho re-mounted, and to rounds of applause and music, they rode to their guide's house, which was large and fine, as befits a rich gentleman.

* * *

Don Quixote's host was Don Antonio Moreno, a wealthy, witty, friendly, honest man, and now the Don was in his house, he tried to think of ways to make the most of his madness, without doing him any harm, because a joke's no joking matter if it hurts, and no distraction distracts, if it damages a third party. The first thing he did was to take off Don Quixote's armour and exhibit him in his pale yellow, tight-fitting doublet on a balcony overlooking one of the city's main streets, in full view of passers-by who gawped at the knight errant as if he were an Easter saffron bun. Once again the liveried riders cantered by, as if they had dressed up for him alone rather than add cheer to that festive day, and Sancho was delighted, thinking he must have chanced upon another wedding, another noble house and another castle like ones they had enjoyed before.

That afternoon they took Don Quixote out for a canter, not in his armour, but wearing a tawny gold cassock that would have made a block of ice sweat. They arranged for their servants to keep Sancho amused in the house. Don Quixote wasn't riding Rocinante, but a large, sure-footed, well-trained mule. Once they'd slipped on the cassock, they sewed a large piece of parchment to the back without him noticing, where they had written in large letters: 'THIS IS DON QUIXOTE FROM LA MANCHA.' The moment they set off, that sign caught the attention of all who had come to see him, and Don Quixote was astonished so many people stared at him and knew him and his name, and he turned to Don Antonio, who was riding next to him, and said: 'Great is the prestige conferred by knight errantry, since it brings fame to the man who professes it on everyone of the earth's frontiers; Don Antonio, just observe how even the youngsters in this city know me, though they can never have seen me before.'

'That's so true, Don Quixote, sir,' replied Don Antonio, 'just as fire cannot be hidden and enclosed, so virtue is always recognized, and much more so when earned from the profession of arms, for then it is honoured above all else.'

And later Don Quixote decided he'd like to go for a quiet stroll and wander in the city, because he was afraid if he went on horseback again, those rude lads might chase him, so he, Sancho, and two of Don Antonio's servants went for a walk.

They were going down a street when Don Quixote looked up and saw emblazoned in very big letters over a doorway, 'Books Printed Here', and he was so happy, because he'd never seen a print-shop before and he wanted to know what one was like. He went inside with his companions, and saw how they laid out pages in one place, corrected in another, set type in another, amended here, as well as all the machines you find in big print-shops. Don Quixote stopped in front of a case and asked what they were doing; the compositor told him, and he was very impressed and walked on. Then he came to another, and asked the tradesman what he was doing. The compositor replied, 'Sir, this gentleman you see here,' and he pointed to a handsome, well-built, rather serious fellow, 'has translated an Italian book into Spanish, and I am setting the pages.'

'What's the book's title?'

'Sir, it's called *Le Bagatelle* in Italian.'

'And what does that mean in Spanish?' asked Don Quixote.

'*Le Bagatelle*', said the author, 'is what we would call "*Los Juguetes*" in Spanish, and although this book has a very modest title, it speaks of fine, substantial things.'

'Well,' said Don Quixote, 'I know a bit of Italian, and I pride myself on being able to recite verse by Ariosto; but tell me, sir, and I don't ask this because I want to test your knowledge, but simply out of curiosity: have you ever come across the word "pignatta" as you translate away?'

'Scores of times,' answered the author.

'And how do you translate it into Spanish?' asked Don Quixote.

'How on earth am I going to translate it, if not by "olla"?' retorted the author.

'Heavens above!' exclaimed Don Quixote, 'You *do* have an advanced knowledge of the Italian language! I'd bet loads of money that when the Italian says "piache", you write "place" in Spanish, and when it says "piu", you put "mas", and "su" for "arriba" and "giu" for "abajo".'

'Yes, of course, I do,' said the author, 'because they are the right meanings.'

'And I'd even dare to bet,' said Don Quixote, 'that nobody has ever heard of you, my good sir, because this world always refuses to recognize real brains or true worth. So many skills are ignored, so many geniuses sidelined, so much talent scorned. Nevertheless, I've always thought that translating from one language to another, if it's not from the regal languages of Latin or Greek, is like looking at the the reverse of a Flemish tapestry; you do see the figures but they are obscured by dangling ends of threads, and you don't get a sense of the smoothness and fullness of the actual tableau and if you're translating from easy languages, you don't need much wit or grasp of words; it's like someone copying or shifting words from one bit of paper to another. And don't think I want to suggest that translating isn't a worthwhile occupation, because a man could do worse things in life that would bring him much less profit. Naturally, I'm not thinking of those two famous translators, Dr Cristobal de Figueroa, and his *Pastor Fido*, or Don Juan Jauregui, and his *Aminta*, where they make you wonder which is the translation and which is the original. But tell me now, are you printing this off your own bat, or have you sold the rights to a bookseller?'

'I'm printing this off my own bat,' replied the author, 'And I expect to earn at least a thousand ducats, at least, from this first edition of two thousand copies, that will sell like hot cakes at six *reales* each.'

'You seem to have done your sums,' replied Don Quixote, 'but it's clear you know nothing about what printers print and sell, and how they report the number of copies sold. I can tell you, when you find you're landed with two thousand copies, you'll be livid. And that's quite likely, if it's on the heavy side, or isn't at all racy.'

'Well, really, what do you expect?' rasped the author, 'Do you expect me to sell the rights to a bookseller for a pittance, though he thinks he's doing me a big favour? I don't print my books to become a name in the land, because I'm that already as a result of my own writing; I want to make money, because without that fame isn't worth a fig.'

'May Lady Luck go with you,' replied Don Quixote.

Then he came to another case, where he saw they were correcting a page of a book called *Light of the Soul* and he immediately exclaimed, 'There are lots of this kind of book, but many more should be printed. There are so many sinners and we need thousands of these little lights for so much darkness.'

He walked on and saw they were revising another book, and asked what its title was and they replied it was *The Second Part of the Ingenious Gentleman Don Quixote*, written by somebody from Tordesillas.

'I've heard about this book,' said Don Quixote, 'and to tell you the honest truth I thought the copies had already been burnt and turned to dust because of the cheek of that fellow, but he'll get his comeuppance soon, because fiction is enjoyable only when it comes close to the truth or something similar, and true ones are all the better for being more truthful.' And, with those words, he stormed angrily out of the printer's.

* * *

And on another afternoon Don Antonio, two friends, and Don Quixote and Sancho went to visit the galleys. The flagship had been warned and prepared a warm welcome for the two celebrities, and the second they stepped on the beach, every galley lifted its mainsail and blew its hornpipes. Then the flagship dropped into the water a skiff, draped with plush rugs and crimson velvet cushions, and when Don Quixote stepped on board, it fired a salvo from its midships cannon and the other galleys followed suit, and when Don Quixote began to climb up the starboard ladder, crew and slaves greeted him, as is the custom when a famous personage boards a galley, shouting: 'Hurrah, hurrah, hurrah' three times. The general—which is what we will call him, as he was an illustrious gentleman from Valencia—shook Don Quixote's hand, embraced him, and declared: 'I shall chalk this day up as one to cherish, the best ever, the day I set eyes on Don Quixote from La

Mancha, that shining symbol of the supreme values of knight errantry.'

Bowled over by such praise, Don Quixote replied with equal grace. They all then walked onto the ornate poop deck and sat on the bulwark benches; the bosun strode down the gangway and a blast from his whistle signalled to the slaves to strip off their rags, which they did in a flash. Sancho was shocked by the sight of all their naked flesh, and even more so when he saw the awnings drop so fast he thought an army of devils must be at work. But that was pancakes soaked in honey compared to what I'll tell you now. Sancho was perched on the seat next to the overseer on the right, who'd received his orders what to do: he grabbed Sancho, lifted him up on his arms, and when the slaves were standing ready, sent him spinning across their arms from bench to bench down his side so fast poor Sancho shut his eyes tight, no doubt reckoning that those same devils were back, who wouldn't stop until they had him whizzed back up the left side and plonked him in the poop. Panting and sweating like a pig, the poor tyke was tottering, quite unable to imagine what had happened.

Don Quixote, who had watched the wingless Sancho in flight, asked the general if that was one of those ceremonies they held for men joining a galley for the first time, because if that were the case, he didn't intend to partake of and experience a similar trial, and swore to God that if anyone tried to grab him and give him a whirl, he'd kick his brains out, and, saying that, he stood up clasping his sword.

Right then they lowered the awnings, and then made a huge din lowering the main mast. Sancho thought the heavens were dropping from their hinges and would collapse on his head, so he stooped and hid it between his knees. Don Quixote was also beside himself; he shuddered, squeezed his shoulders inwards, while his face turned a deathly pale. The slaves then hoisted the mast as fast and noisily as they had lowered it, although they said nothing, because they owned neither voice nor breath. The bosun signalled for the anchor to be raised and, leaping into amidships, began to beat the backs of the slaves with his whip or scourge as the galley slowly sailed out to sea. When Sancho saw so many dark feet moving, he thought they must be oars, and muttered to himself: 'These are truly enchanted things and not those my master talks about, and why does that one man who keeps blowing his whistle dare whip so many people? I reckon I must be in hell, or at least in purgatory.'

Don Quixote noticed how closely Sancho was following events, and said: 'Ah, Sancho, my friend, if you wanted, you could quickly, and at little cost to yourself, strip to your waist, and seat yourselves among these gentlemen and put an end to the enchantment of my Dulcinea! As so many are suffering and sorrowing, you'd hardly feel your own pain, and, besides, it might be that wise magician Merlin might consider each lash, delivered with such a thwack, worth ten of what you really ought to receive.'

The general wanted to ask what lashes he meant, or what on earth disenchanting Dulcinea was all about, when the pilot shouted: 'Montjuí is signalling there's a vessel off the coast to the west.'

Hearing that, the general jumped amidships and said: 'Hey, lads, give chase! The lookout must be warning us of a pirate brig from Algiers.'

Then the three other galleys sailed up to the flagship to get their orders. The general ordered two to take to the open sea, and the other to accompany him along the coast, that way the vessel could never escape. The slaves gripped their oars and drove the galleys so frantically they seemed to fly through the water. The two that sailed two miles out to sea spotted the brig with fourteen or fifteen benches of slaves rowing, then saw it turn to make a quick escape, which was a waste of time, because the flagship was one of the fleetest on the ocean and soon caught up. Those aboard the brig realized they couldn't escape and their Moorish skipper told them to stop rowing and not provoke the captain of the galleys. But Lady Luck, who'd planned things differently, ensured that the flagship sailed so close they could hear the voices demanding they surrender, and two *toraquis or* drunken Turks, who were with twelve others, shot and killed two of our soldiers in the forecastle. Then the general swore to kill every man on the brig, but attacked in such a frenzy it managed to get away. The galley shot forwards and those in the brig gave themselves up for lost but then did raise their sail and row out of danger, though their derring-do was futile and did them harm, because after a half-mile pursuit the flagship caught up and took everyone prisoner.

The two other galleys appeared, and all four escorted the captured vessel to the beach in Barcelona where crowds were waiting, eager to see what their catch was. The general anchored near land and noticed the city's viceroy on the seafront. He sent the skiff to get him and ordered the mast be lowered so they could hang the skipper and the other Turks they'd taken captive from the brig, thirty-six all told, all rippling muscle and mostly Turkish musketeers. The general asked who their skipper was, and one man replied in Spanish (who later seemed to be a renegade Spaniard): 'Sir, this lad you see here is our skipper.'

And he pointed to one of the most handsome, graceful young men the human imagination could have ever portrayed. He looked under twenty.

'Tell me, dog, what led you to kill my soldiers when you saw you were never going to escape? Why did you show such disrespect for my flagship? Can't you tell the difference between rashness and courage? Faint hope should make men daring, but never rash.'

The skipper began to reply, but the general couldn't listen because he had to welcome the viceroy who was boarding the galley with his entourage of servants and townspeople.

'A good haul!' said the viceroy.

'And it will look even finer', replied the general, 'when Your Excellency sees them hanging from that mast.'

'Why so?' retorted the viceroy.

'Because, defying every law, the conventions of war and good sense,' the general answered, 'they killed two of the best soldiers sailing in my galleys, and I have sworn to hang every prisoner, starting with this youngster, the brig's skipper.'

He pointed to the youth who was awaiting his death, his hands already tied and a noose around his neck.

The viceroy glanced at him, and the sight of a youth so handsome, graceful, and shy, was so like a glowing letter of introduction he decided he didn't want him to die. He asked: 'Tell me, skipper, were you born a Turk, a Moor or are you a renegade Spaniard?'

The young man replied in Spanish: 'I am neither a native Turk, a Moor, or a renegade Spaniard.'

'So what are you?' enquired the viceroy.

'A Christian woman,' replied the young man.

'A woman, a Christian, in those clothes and doing these things? That is cause for astonishment rather than belief.'

'Good sirs,' cried the youngster, 'call off the execution, for your hunger for revenge will soon grow cold when you hear the story of my life.'

Who could be so hard-hearted they wouldn't be softened by such a plea, or at least feel they should hear what the sad, pitiful young man had to relate?

The general told him to speak his mind, but not to expect forgiveness for his evident guilt.

With that go-ahead, the lad began to speak: 'I was born of *morisco* parents, from that nation, that is unhappy rather than prudent, and has suffered the onslaught of a storm of misfortunes.* Fleeing their hapless fate, an uncle and aunt of mine took me to North Africa where it wasn't at all sensible to say I was a Christian girl, which is in effect what I am, and not the sort that pretend and simulate, but the true Catholic kind. Telling the truth to those responsible for our wretched exile was no help either, and my aunt and uncle also refused to believe me, they thought I had lied so I could stay in the land of my birth, and thus, more by force of circumstance than pleasure, they took me with them. My mother was Christian and my father was a Christian too and a decent man; I suckled the Catholic faith with my

* 'Morisco' is the name given to Muslims who remained in Spain after decrees issued in the first quarter of the sixteenth century ordered them to convert to Catholicism or leave the country. Most stayed on and practised their religion secretly. King Philip III decreed their expulsion on 9 April 1609. Historians estimate that over half a million left Spain, though many returned and were assimilated.

mother's milk, I was brought up to be well-mannered, and, as I see it, I have never acted as a *morisca* in my speech or behaviour. Alongside these virtues (which is what I truly think they are), my beauty flowered, if I may say that, and although I was well-behaved and rarely went out, that didn't suffice, because I caught the attention of a young gentleman, Don Gaspar Gregorio, the eldest son of a gentleman from a neighbouring village. It would take far too long to tell you how he came to see me, how we spoke, how he became enraptured, how I wasn't so won over by him, particularly when I fear the rough rope that threatens to come between my tongue and throat. I will simply add that Don Gregorio decided to accompany me into exile. He mingled with the *moriscos* who departed from other villages, because he was fluent in their language, and on the journey he befriended my aunt and uncle, because my cautious, prudent father had left our village as soon as he heard our exile proclaimed and had gone in search of someone in foreign kingdoms who might give us refuge. He boxed up and buried in a place only known to me valuable pearls and precious stones, including gold doubloons and silver coins. He ordered me not to touch that treasure, unless they banished us before he returned. I obeyed him, and with my aunt and uncle, other relatives and friends we journeyed to North Africa, and established ourselves in Algiers, as if that city were hell on earth. Their king heard of my beauty, and fame spread news of my wealth, which was lucky for me too up to a point. He summoned me into his presence and asked me which part of Spain I was from and if I had brought money and jewels. I told him the name of our village, that the jewels and money were buried there, and could easily be recovered if I returned for them. I told him this, fearful he would be blinded by my beauty, and not by his desire for those riches.

'While we were conversing, he was informed that I'd been accompanied by one of the most handsome, refined young men imaginable. I realized immediately they were referring to Don Gaspar Gregorio, whose beauty surpassed any other that might be named. I was worried, realizing the danger Don Gregorio was in, because those wild Turks prefer to love a handsome lad or youth rather that any woman, however beautiful she may be. The king ordered them to bring him into his presence so he could see for himself, and he asked me if what they'd said about the young man was true. As if I'd been blessed by a sudden insight sent from heaven, I said he was, but that I must confess that he wasn't male, but female like myself, and begged him to let me dress her in her rightful clothes, to show off her beauty, and appear in his presence with less embarrassment. He agreed and said we'd talk some other day about how to organize my return to Spain to reclaim that hidden treasure.

'I spoke to Don Gaspar and told him the danger he ran if he dressed as a male. I dressed him like a Moorish girl, and that same afternoon took him into the presence of the king, who was immediately struck by her, and planned to keep her so he could give her as a present to the Grand Sultan, and to avoid the danger he might face in his own harem—because he didn't trust himself—he ordered her to be taken to the house of a prominent Moorish lady who would look after her, and he was taken there at once.

'The sadness we felt, for I won't deny that I love him, I will leave to the imagination of those who have been separated from those they love each other deeply. The king ordered me to return to Spain in this brig accompanied by the two native Turks who killed your soldiers. This renegade Spaniard came as well—she pointed to the man who had spoken first—whom I know is really a clandestine Christian who wants to stay in Spain rather than return to North Africa; the rest are Moorish or Turkish slaves who are only fit to row. Those two uncouth, greedy Turks didn't obey the order to leave this renegade and me in Spain dressed in the Christian clothes we'd brought with us, but decided to sweep the coast and plunder what they could. They were afraid that if they left us on land, and if something happened to us, their brig would be spotted out to sea, and if there were galleys on the coast, they might be taken prisoner. Last night we found this beach in Barcelona, and unaware of the presence of your four galleys, we were discovered, and you all saw what happened. In conclusion, Don Gregorio remains among women, dressed as a woman, in clear danger of losing his life, and I'm here with my hands tied, waiting or, rather fearing I will lose mine, which I'm mightily tired of anyway. Gentlemen, this is the end of my sad story, as true as it is unhappy: I beg you to let me die a Christian, for, as I have said, I am not at all responsible for the guilt assigned to the people of my nation.'

And she fell silent, tender tears welled in her eyes, and in those of many present. The compassionate viceroy said nothing, walked over, and removed the rope binding the beautiful Moorish woman's hands.

While the Christian *morisca* recounted her strange tale, an aged pilgrim who had boarded the boat along with the viceroy kept his eyes glued on her, and she had barely finished when he threw himself at her feet and exclaimed, interrupting his flow with a thousand sobs and sighs: 'Oh, Ana Félix, my long-lost daughter! I am Ricote your father, who has just returned to look for you, because I can't live without you, my love.'

When Sancho heard that, he looked up (for he'd been looking down, still thinking about how he'd been whirled up and down the ship), and, looking at the pilgrim, he recognized him as that very same Ricote he had met the day he left the island he was governing. And now it had been confirmed that girl was his daughter, who, freed from her fetters, embraced her father, mingling her tears with his. Ricote spoke to the general and viceroy: 'My dear sirs, this is my daughter who is more wretched in life than in name: Ana Félix is her name, Ricote her surname, renowned as much for her beauty as for my wealth. I left my land to search in foreign parts for someone who would welcome and give us refuge, and, after finding such a person in Germany, I returned in this pilgrim garb, accompanied by other Germans, to look for my daughter and dig up the precious treasure I had buried. I didn't find my daughter: I did find the treasure I have with me now, but in these strange circumstances you have all witnessed, I have now discovered the treasure that most enriches me. If our lack of guilt and her tears and mine, and the righteousness of your justice, can open the gates to mercy, please show us mercy, because we never thought to offend, nor did we ever agree with the intentions of our people who have rightly been exiled.'

Then Sancho spoke: 'I know Ricote well and what he says about Ana Félix being his daughter is true, though

I won't get mixed up in the petty details of all that to-and-froing or those good or bad intentions.'

All present wondered at the strangeness of that case and the general said: 'Your tears prevent me from carrying out my oath: beautiful Ana Félix, live the years of life heaven has granted you, and may that insolent, rash pair be sentenced as guilty for the crimes they committed.'

And he ordered the two Turks who had killed his soldiers be hung from the mast, but the viceroy passionately begged him not to do so, because their acts had been acts of rashness rather than courage. The general agreed to the viceroy's request, because cold-blooded vengeance is never a good idea. Then they tried to organize the rescue of Don Gaspar Gregorio from the danger he was facing; Ricote offered over two thousand ducats he was carrying in pearls and jewels. Many offered other support, but none like the man who'd been described a renegade Spaniard, who offered to return to Algiers in a small craft, with up to six benches of Christian oarsmen, because he knew where, how, and when he could and should disembark and was likewise familiar with the house where Don Gaspar was lodged. The general and viceroy hesitated, unsure they could trust the renegade or his Christian rowers; Ana Félix backed him, and her father Ricote said he would go to the rescue of the Christians if they were taken captive.

After deciding on this plan of action, the viceroy disembarked and Don Antonio Moreno took the *morisca* and her father to his house, and the viceroy ordered him to cherish and cosset them as much as he could, and he, for his part, offered him gifts of whatever he wanted from his own residence, so much good will and charity had Ana Félix's beauty aroused in his heart.

Transplanted

Narcís Oller

1

Daniel, or Friar Baker, as everyone called him, was happy in his village and thought nothing in this world could be lovelier: he had toiled hard and long from a young age, and watched his beads of sweat turn into the gold or silver coins his wife put away in the drawer, not as units of exchange but as so many badges of honour.

Because of his unshakeable happiness, or perhaps because even the smell of flour is nourishing, he had always been robust and had now become so rotund and paunchy it was almost pitiful. And I say 'almost' because the healthy colour of his cheeks, his tranquil gaze, and the permanent smile on his lips displayed such contentment and well being it was impossible to sustain the feeling of pity his bloated appearance inspired at first glance.

No concerns, no quarrels with life, no sense of unease: the happiness of Friar Baker was proverbial in the village and surrounding countryside.

Of course, by the age of sixty, he hadn't been spared the grief that pursues every mortal, such as family losses, including his wife's painful decease, but all such sorrow, even the saddest, were short lived for Daniel, thanks to his own doughy character that was far superior to what he put in the bread he baked, and to the *philosophy* and *religion* he drew on in those situations.

He always had a friendly word for everyone, and nobody ever walked past him without greeting him or asking if he was 'enjoying the fresh air', or 'the sunshine', or 'if he was having a rest'.

Popularity, the aspiration of so many, was Friar Baker's soft spot, and he curried it with all his might, appealing to the good will of poor and rich alike, flattering, and never insulting anyone.

That's never easy in any social sphere of life, and particularly hard in a tiny village, but, as instinct is all, and Daniel had more than enough in that respect, and seemed to have patented blandness, he effortlessly got what he wanted. That was why he was on good terms with Dr Andreu, the cleverest man thereabouts, who dazzled all the villagers with the chunks of history, geography, or astronomy he rattled off the moment he had memorized them, accompanied by the proverbs and worldly wisdom that, like a second Sancho Panza, he casually dropped into the conversation.

In one of these lectures, as Dr Andreu called them, because they were undeniably educational, he said: 'a wise man soon becomes a donkey in a village of dimwits'.

When he said that, I'm not sure whether he was thinking he himself had mentally declined or that some of his audience might once have been sage. Nor do I know whether Daniel had any reason to feel badly done by in the village of his birth where he had been blissfully baking bread and hoarding gold. However, what I do know is that the human mind is prone to strange twists and, as a result, Dr Andreu's words of wisdom perhaps set our innocent baker thinking, and from then on, he cherished a desire to leave his village one day and go, as one might say, in search of new horizons. In the end, I know that, thanks to this ambition, Daniel was overjoyed to see his elder son go off to Barcelona to learn the trade of hairdressing, even though his departure was a source of anguish, and broke the usual custom of an heir routinely following in his father's footsteps. Perhaps that upstanding fellow thought his son would soak up knowledge through his fingers combing the hair of a professor or one of those distinguished gentlemen who are an authority on this or that, and like to display their crosses and insignia!

Be that as it may, Friar Baker's son served his apprenticeship in Barcelona, and, in the period we are referring to, opened his own salon, investing a goodly part of the 'badges of honour' his mother had hoarded in its installations and decor.

The launching of the hairdressing salon was too much of a landmark to take place in the absence of his father, and, naturally, the son went to bring him to Barcelona, a city he had never visited.

The salon was on La Rambla, and the solemn inauguration took place the day after they arrived. It wasn't simply nice; it was sumptuous. Miquelet, who in the industrial world bore the battle name of *Lavish*, was cannier than his mentor Figaro. He had grasped the spirit of the times and knowing that nowadays expenditure paid dividends, he decided not to skimp. Then he felt elated he had mounted a salon that was unique in Spain, and thought his next step must be to make a splash in the daily newspapers, and, following the example set by other enterprises, he decided to offer a dinner to the representatives of the press, as they are now called.

He and his father had arrived in Barcelona the previous night. We have mentioned it was the first visit by Daniel who had never visited *any* city of a similar size. One can see this from his first impressions, which were a hundred times more stunning than any child might experience. A child wouldn't have the criteria to grasp the true value of such new perceptions or knowledge beyond what he had seen with his own eyes to compare to what he was witnessing for the first time.

A few kilometres before they arrived, Daniel couldn't decide what on earth he was seeing as he contemplated strings of lights he sometimes saw whole and at others in part, depending on the bends or level of the train track. No citizen of Barcelona ever sees the city as huge as it appears to the eyes of an outsider. Friar Baker's son did his best to to encourage that sensation.

'Father, do you see that line of different coloured lights on the left? That's Passeig de Gràcia.* The other streets crossing it are streets in the Ensanche . . . Look to the right: that long row of lights is a single road: the road to Sants. Montjuic is further up . . . Can you see it now the moon has come out from behind those big clouds? Do you see that other big glow, further down, in the distance? That's the sea . . . Look how beautiful it is now the moon is shining on it! It's like a lake of shimmering silver!'

* At the time, the Martorell line, after Sants, had its terminus at the start of the Ronda de la Universitat by the Plaça de Catalunya, where the station once stood. It didn't cross the Passeig de Gràcia, as it does today, nor did it stop in the Estació de França. (Author's note.)

Daniel looked left and right, up and down, at the ground and at the sky, and felt almost dizzy. A wall, a house, a dip in the track, the speed of the train made the lights flicker so oddly and anxiously he sometimes mistook them for the stars and lost all notion of sky and earth.

'Come over here. Now you can see lots of lights!'

Daniel's eyes were like dinner plates.

'If it was daytime, I'd show you Pedralbes, Sarrià, Vallvidrera, Sant Gervasi, Gràcia; it's one mass of houses . . . We'll soon be there . . . Look, that's the Sarrià train! Look at that bridge crossing above the track: another train will pass over our heads.'

By now the baker's head was spinning and he could hardly grasp how it would pass over them without crushing them, and was about to cross himself.

Finally the train whistled, stopped and porters came to collect tickets, dazzling the passengers with the bright, flashing light of their lanterns.

Meanwhile, Daniel followed his son's pointing finger and observed the ugly pile that was the University, that, shrouded in darkness, seemed like a gigantic parapet flanked by two big towers.

'Did you see that thin spire further down? It's a nunnery: Les Adoratrices. We also passed Les Arrepentides, Sant Joan de Déu, and other convents. The place is full of them. Those friars and nuns know what they're about: this is the southern corner . . . Now we're on the move again: the engine is pushing us from behind now. Stand up. Do you see those four lines of lights? That's the Gran Via, a road that goes on forever.'

The brakes began to squeal, the wheels to drag.

'We've arrived,' said *Lavish*, sticking his flat cap in his pocket and donning an extremely elegant bowler. 'Watch out and careful with your timepiece, there are some prying fingers around here . . .'

Words can't describe the baker's impressions as he crossed La Rambla. The coloured lights of carriages moving in different directions, the people seated in trams, the flood of light from shops, the huddles of window-shoppers, the crowd strolling under the trees, the bright publicity hoardings; everything seemed strange in his eyes and made him dizzy.

He thought Barcelona was heaven because of the lights and hell because of the din. He couldn't decide if he did or didn't like it: he wanted to get to his son's, yet at the same time would have preferred not to arrive there too quickly.

He found such mental confusion exhausting. So, after supper, when he went to bed, he sighed contentedly, shut his eyes, and tried to sleep. It was hopeless: his mind was in turmoil, a law unto itself, and dead set on not resting. If he opened his eyes, he thought he could see through the darkness the top and bottom corners of the bedroom sink and rise, as if he were in a ship's cabin subject to the perpetual seesaw of the ocean waves. If he shut them, he saw a swarm of multicoloured lights flying in a huge constellation that ignored every law of physics. Daniel didn't know what to do on that bed of torture and thought more than once that he should get up. Finally, drowsiness overcame his anxiety, the bedroom was enveloped by an impenetrable, pitch-black silence, the pinpoints of light shrank into thin pale yellow threads, and Daniel's mind gradually slipped down the gentle slope of sleep where all sense of existence vanishes.

The following day wasn't any less of an emotional rollercoaster. Morning and afternoon he strolled through Barcelona, in awe, stopping in front of every shop window or at a respectful distance from the vehicles he saw rushing towards him.

The view of the sea, with its forest of masts and rigging, almost hid the endless bustle on the wharves; luxury carriages with gold-braided lackeys drawn by pairs of proud horses; Plaça Reial, with its perfect elegance and symmetry; La Rambla, with its cheerful bustle; and Passeig de Gràcia, full of life and movement. Daniel was bewitched by it all.

However, even if you combined all those daytime impressions, they were nothing compared to what awaited him at that evening's inauguration.

Daniel could hardly credit the sight of his son among all those representatives of the press, their eyes travelling from walls to table as they waited for their supper, and showered their host with praise for the wealth of good taste he had invested in his establishment, promising him a splendid future. They inspected and lauded the mirrors, lighting, and dressing tables, and, especially, the oils, pomades, essences, and cosmetics of English origins (a novelty the new barber had introducing to enhance his standing).

Lavish simply had to react at that point: in a highly charged gesture he signalled to an apprentice to wrap up the phials and pots that had received the most plaudits, even though it ruined the perfect symmetry and abundance the shelves had displayed at the start of the soirée.

Friar Baker almost shed tears of joy. His son *was* a wise man and Dr Andreu was right to say that 'a wise man soon becomes a donkey in a village of dimwits'. Back there, whenever would his Miquelet have rubbed shoulders with so many men of letters or learned to do so with such confidence and familiarity? The old man's insight, that he had rarely ever exercised, began to sense the hidden vein of self-interest his son was mining with the subtle savoir-faire of a courtier or, if you prefer, of an entrepreneur in the contemporary world. His father was just cottoning on, while his son was scaling the heights.

In the course of dinner (that, as you will imagine, had been made the responsibility of a gourmet restaurant, though it was being served in a hairdressing salon), conversation took off slowly, but quickened when the meat and wine made the assembled brains bubble and eventually explode the moment the champagne bottles were uncorked.

Without blinking an eyelid, as if to the manner born, the hairdresser raised his glass and launched into a speech, in which he elevated 'the press, the voice of public opinion, the great lever of progress', above all the great and the good on this earth. 'Because,' he said, 'you are unique in the way you combine to encourage every enterprise, however modest. The press treats invitations from the Palace the same as one from a humble business chap like me: it scorns nobody, and offers the same confraternity that exists among all its representatives, without party prejudice, to all social classes.'

The diners clapped heartily. The baker wept and laughed simultaneously.

Then the journalists began their round of toasts. On behalf of the press (not just of Barcelona, or Spain, but of *the whole world*), one thanked the hairdresser for his eulogies of 'the greatest institution of our era'. Another tried to demonstrate that there was no human action, however insignificant, that wasn't of use in the construction of progress, adding that, as a result, the press, 'as the proprietor of this establishment has said most eloquently', never denies its support to the smallest of enterprises, though he cavilled, 'one can hardly describe a hairdressing salon as paltry, in which the art of adornment, distilled by good taste, converges with the art of the haircut, polishing and perfecting the profiles of civilized men so they can never, ever, even from a distance, be mistaken for savages.'

Friar Baker's brain now boiled to the point of explosion.

Using statistical data he had memorized, another journalist revealed that in the civilized world there was only one hairdresser for every fifty thousand men, and that, even though such an imbalance didn't exist in Barcelona, he could unambiguously declare that the service had been underexploited and this new salon would soon welcome a massive clientele.

His final word inspired another toast, when it was argued that the art of haircutting and combing lay at the very heart of Catholicism, as could be deduced from the various hairstyles favoured by friars and the edicts of excommunication the Church had published in times of yore against certain exaggerated hair arrangements that, in England and other nations, bestowed a monstrous appearance on both men and women. The orator then alleged that the inauguration of a hairdressing salon couldn't, quite frankly, be devoid of importance or interest for all those students of the essence of civilization who were of a mind that each new concern contributed towards progress and was *a very good thing*.

I can hardly express what passed through the good baker's mind. 'I could never have dreamed of this! I was surrounded by men far wiser than Dr Andreu! And it was Miquelet who had brought them together, who had flattered and been praised in return! My son, o Lord, my son!'

Daniel now nourished the slight hope that he too might become known to that enlightened coterie. He reviewed that spectacle of those individuals now mingling and fraternizing through rose-tinted spectacles and was transported to realms of the utmost naivete. He remembered Dr Andreu's barbed quip and reckoned it had never been more apposite. He felt his whole village deserved the utmost pity. 'To live in Barcelona was to live to the full.' What he had seen during the day and was seeing now was a dream tempting him to make it his perpetual reality. 'I've made my mind up: in my old age I should become a citizen of Barcelona.' He suddenly longed to live amongst *celebrities*, and, feeling he too was on the ascent, he decided he would offer a toast.

At the other end of the table, *Lavish*'s studied smile concealed his fear that his father might be an embarrassment. Everyone went quiet, all eyes sought a place to focus above his napkin. The silence intimidated the new orator before he even opened his lips, but, having committed himself, he now wanted to speak from the heart.

'Gentlemen,' Daniel finally began, 'I am very gratified, terribly so . . . and I offer a toast to the health of you and your families . . . and I will say no more . . . because I can't.'

And he slumped on his chair like a ton of lead, tears welling in his eyes, while his audience rose to their feet as a man and applauded him as they wet their lips with champagne.

Two or three more speeches from other journalists crowned a night of monumental oratory, and, before coffee was served, the big surprise *Lavish* had secretly prepared had its moment.

It was an elegantly Etruscan, white metal, lidded urn. Located at the centre of the table, everybody had assumed it was a mere decorative item destined to enhance the display of flowers, candelabra, glasses, bottles, and cutlery that reflected the gaslight and broke into myriad colours vying in their brightness and animation. However, that was not the purpose of that urn.

Miquelet stood up, pressed the button on the top of the lid, and a hundred spouts (so small they were invisible) spurted a hundred jets of aromatic fragrance freshening the atmosphere and filling the salon with a delightful scent.

I can't begin to describe how they applauded that device: the whole gathering clapped and shivered in pleasure, aping the sybaritic *frissons* of Romans during the late Empire as they were tickled by that gentle spray of enervating vapours.

The steamy aroma from the coffee and the circles of cigar smoke rose to the ceiling; the candles diffused a whiter, wan light; gas-lit globes took on a bluish hue; and every diner subsided into a mood of relaxed, soporific well being.

Without exception, the next morning's dailies portrayed the new hairdressing salon as if it were a fairy palace, praising all the innovations imported by *Lavish*, and listing the entrepreneurs who had contributed to the decor, although they made a mess of some of the names and attributes.

2

The scenes described above, and the good life Miquelet was forging for himself, fired Daniel's desire to rent out his bakery and spend the rest of his days in Barcelona. He had toiled long enough; nobody could criticize him for retiring at what was a respectable old age. His savings allowed him to, and, besides, his son had willingly offered him a place at his table and a comfortable bed.

Daniel returned to the village where he had lived happily for so many years with that aim in his sights. If he hadn't arrived with such a longing to uproot, he might perhaps have shaken off the despondency he felt as he trod those streets again.

It was autumn, and he arrived after nightfall.

Those who have only experienced village life in summer cannot imagine the gloom it brings on at the onset of winter, and how that gloom deepens as the sun hides behind the mountains.

The first swift to leave a village is the precursor of solitude and silence. It is followed by others, emptying nests, once warm and full of life, that now crumble with the rain and the wind. Farmhouses are shut up, the handful of luxury carriages and broughams put into store, soon to be covered by dust and cobwebs; horse-driven charabancs struggle to transport back to the city all the visitors who have injected life into the village and countryside for three months. There is an end to partying by the fountain, to dancing, to local festivities, bustle, and good cheer: life retreats back within four walls and roads and paths will soon solely be the wind's domain.

When Friar Baker turned down his street, it was past twilight. He no longer found groups of people enjoying the fresh air, or saw the carpenter's shop open, tools in place, floor washed, and dining-room balcony window bathed in the glimmering light from an oil lamp.

Everything was shut up without a soul in sight, and a starry expanse of turquoise blue sky extended over the crooked roofs like a tattered canopy. In that solitude he heard the jack plane slide, the saw scrape, and the carpenter's hammer thud.

Those noises dimmed when they reached Daniel's heart: a vague association of ideas made him think the carpenter was making a coffin.

Ten steps further on, a hammer rang out on an anvil like a distant bell, and, through a shutter in the stairway,

Daniel saw his neighbour, a blacksmith, in a red glow from a star of sparks that, as he hammered, stretched or shrunk its points like a tortured hedgehog of fire.

Daniel pushed the unsightly bakery door, and saw the oven's flaming mouth, flames that leapt through the air and licked the narrow door of their prison, as if to greet their returning master. The bakery filled with joy. Everybody left their tasks and surrounded him, and he didn't know which way to turn or how to answer the hundred questions suddenly directed at him.

When he reached his flat and looked out of the window, as if driven by an odious desire to make comparisons, the street was at its bleakest. The wind howled along the ground sending up winged phantoms of dust, darkness hid the fronts of houses, and only the faintest lullaby sung by a mother cradling her child, together with the dim chanting of seamstresses and the noisy clatter of a door bolt, broke that silence of the graveyard.

Daniel felt depressed. The whole of Barcelona was buzzing around his head, and he duly scrutinized that dismal street seeking the delights he had found there throughout his life.

'At least let's have some moonlight!' he muttered. Frankly, he was longing for the rivers of light that flooded the big city when night fell: the resplendent gleam of the hairdresser's, the Venetian lights of carriages and trams he watched from his son's balcony, as they capriciously sped and swerved.

One doesn't need much of a taste: once one's eyes have enjoyed a good dose of artificial light, one soon misses it. Just imagine what our baker must have been thinking, a man who had experienced a place where everything glittered, where everything reflected the brightness of a hundred gas flames, from the black top hats of his son's customers to the floor tiles.

He was now sure he couldn't possibly live happily in that dark, dirty, remote village. He recalled the press dinner, Dr Andreu's quip, the progress made by Miquelet, the things he had offered, his promise that he would now accept, the reasons why it was time for him to relax... shut his window, then climbed into bed, more determined than ever to leave.

3

Daniel easily rented out his bakery: though not now because he was so keen to forsake its walls; after his initial enthusiasm, his memories of Barcelona had begun to fade, and once again those walls warmed his heart and expressed the history of an existence he had suddenly scorned for no good reason. However, his mind was made up: the bakery was rented and all he had left in the village was a married daughter, in whose house he did not live... 'I will be close to my son, I will hobnob with the famous, and a thousand distractions will help me to pass my time that I'll find intolerable here, now I'm not working. Besides, I can come back in the summer. And what if I never see my home again? Well, I can do without it.'

His eyes sparkled and he plucked up courage; days before he had felt so grim when he had returned to his village but now he left feeling infinite regret.

However, Daniel's huge frame was home to a childish temperament that, as with most of his contemporaries, felt more attracted to frivolous gaiety than to melancholy. That's why, when he saw the strings of lights that heralded his return to the big city, he soon forgot the poetry of his home and bakery, and again decided he'd made the obvious choice between what he was forsaking and what the city had to offer. Poor Daniel forgot that Barcelona couldn't supply new treats every day, and that, at a certain age, force of habit is all powerful.

He had already strolled around most of the city on his first stay; his son was busy in his salon and couldn't keep him company, and, if idle loafers baulked at living twenty-four hours a day on their savings, a man like him so used to hard work might soon find himself in a worse pickle.

He began to feel the effects the day after he'd arrived. Accustomed to rising early when the kneaders had prepared a supply of dough, he woke up at his usual time, that was far too early for a hairdresser's, and, as he was no longer a visitor from the sticks and didn't want to stop waking up early, he jumped out of bed. The dawn light was enough for the baker to get dressed, and his fingers identified each piece of the suit draped over the backs of chairs as if they were pale coloured cloths. Everyone else in the house would sleep for another three hours, and the warmth and quiet reigning over the bedrooms made him tiptoe and hold his breath. On the other hand, he didn't know where the keys to the flat or the door to the street were, and couldn't make his way to the street. If one day you find yourself in that state, trapped in a bedroom with only the window to an inside yard for relief, you will realize how Daniel was suffering and will be sympathetic to his sadness that morning.

As he once asked his village for the moon, he now asked the city for the sun.

'Everything is such a struggle!' he muttered. And as he couldn't stand being incarcerated like that and wasn't prepared to wake up the others, he walked across the flat and opened the door to one of the balconies that looked down on La Rambla in order to find a distraction while he waited for the others to get out of bed.

Bleary-eyed gaslighters were extinguishing the wan yellow flames that seemed tired of glimmering; the odd closed carriage, the odd empty cart, the odd individual jaywalker on the empty road were all the movement there was on the Rambla whose bustle the night he'd arrived had made Daniel feel so dizzy. However, the ashen veil stretching from the port to the mountain gradually retreated to the latter, chased by a fresh wind that could have aroused the sleepiest giant. The few green leaves on the trees perked up, and their branches rustled and dusted off their drowsiness; under the bluest sky the spikes of lightning conductors, the metal and glass of belfries and turrets twinkled like bright stars, and a growing hum of people and carriages began to surge from every corner like bees swarming in the hive.

A little later, apprentice barbers started cleaning the salon with dusters, sweeping with their brooms, washing its face and sprucing it up; in a word, they got it ready to welcome the first customers of the morning.

When the baker came downstairs, *Lavish* was still asleep, though his salon was spick and span with the poise of a gentleman who cherishes his dignity and never wants a single soul, however early he rises, to catch him unawares.

I won't claim that Daniel spent the day in a state of anger or boredom: the contrast between Barcelona's lively streets and his silent, deserted village still struck him, though not as much as on his first visit. Buildings and shops no longer seemed novel. He almost knew by heart what he was going to find to his right or left when he turned down a main street or into a big square, and was forced to wander off to unfamiliar districts to find new sights and sounds, or else stop and gawp at one of the spectacles that always attract idlers, however often they have seen them: the tooth-pullers, the birds of fortune, the blind orchestra of Sant Gaietà, the monkeys clambering up balconies, and so many other acts that after two days he knew better than any local.

He managed to have a reasonably entertaining month: one day visiting the Barceloneta, another Montjuic castle, or going to Pedralbes or Can Tunis or Vallcarca or la Bonanova (in a word rambling to pastures new), but even so Daniel couldn't relax. Somehow he had lost the good cheer he had felt for so many years: however sunny it was, however beautiful things were, they always seemed obscured by a mysterious shadow that annoyed rather than amused. He recalled the village and his past life, and tried to persuade himself to go back to that. At other times he remembered the banquet with the journalists, thought of the future his son was forging and felt a new ray of hope and happiness lighten his spirit. But when he arrived home after a four- or five-hour silent and lonely stroll, and was forced to sit in the lobby like a concierge, or else in the dining room, unable to converse with anyone, Friar Baker sank back into a swamp of despondency.

He really didn't know what was happening, and couldn't get to the bottom of his malaise.

'Don't you eat well, sleep well, don't you enjoy more freedom and independence? Doesn't your son treat you well? Shouldn't you be pleased to see how his business is thriving? Aren't you where you wanted to be for so long?'

All his responses were positive . . . and yet he still felt restless.

That sense of abandonment he had felt on his first morning was soon addressed by his son who provided Daniel with a set of keys so he could come and go as he pleased, and one by one his son dealt with all the grouses his father voiced. Every day he tried to show him new walks, and on evenings when he wasn't busy, he accompanied him to a theatre or bar, when his father wanted to go, which was rarely, because he preferred to go to sleep in bed than doze off in public.

4

One night Daniel came back cock-a-hoop: he had bumped into someone from his village and they had spoken at length about the goings-on there. It was the first time, apart from the few outings with his son, that he had strolled around the city deep in conversation. His usual silence amid the crowd was one of the things he found most dispiriting. He remembered how everyone in his village used to greet him, and couldn't adapt to mingling with thousands and thousands of people like a blank cipher.

That was why Daniel found the icy silence amid the madding crowd so much sadder than the quiet solitude around his bakery. Often his legs guided him instinctively to solitary locations; one day his son asked him why and his father replied he found the constant bustle depressing, that the centre of Barcelona felt like a cemetery where only the dead walked.

The fellow villager thought Daniel seemed gloomy and that his hair was greyer; it was 'as if he'd shrunk or put on a straitjacket'. He also noted that when he talked about Barcelona, he hardly listened, and only cheered up when he gossiped about the village, asking after everyone and everything that had happened since his departure, even shedding a tear when he informed him about the births and deaths. His observations were much debated in the village and were attributed to a fallout between father or son by some, to an onset of angina by others.

At night Daniel dreamt of his village. First, he saw himself with Roser, his wife; they were walking across the cemetery overgrown with long grass entangled with wild roses and wisteria that twined around the few crosses there were; then he saw a jet-black sky where a host of stars twinkled nonstop, and, just as he had gone from the brightest sun to the blackest night, he found himself, quite inexplicably, back in his house, wearing a nightshirt and holding a shovel in front of an oven that blazed like a slice of the sun. The glow from the oven shone on the flagstones like a luminous circle projected by a magic lantern, and Daniel could see his own body at its centre, shrinking or lengthening depending on the restless ebb and flow of the flames, monstrously imitating the contortions he was performing with the shovel. Meanwhile, inside the oven, the bread swelled and baked like beans in fertile soil. It soon turned golden, and Daniel was a sight to behold as he manoeuvred the bread onto the shovel and pulled it towards him through the river of flames that was competing for his prey.

At that point, a muffled scream shattered the solemn quiet of the bedroom. Daniel turned on his side and a gentle smile hovered on his lips; the last farewell from the bliss that had visited him that day. Then . . . his spirit enjoyed a deep slumber.

As he woke up, his eyes stared for a moment at the gallery over the inside yard, and a shame-faced tear slid down his cheek.

Then Daniel wondered how long it was to summer. It was only January: five months seemed like a century. However, as desire for solace engendered fresh hopes, some came: if he went down to the station, he would see someone else from his village.

Daniel didn't reflect how it was located in the province of Tarragona and five hours by train, and that his neighbours only came to the Catalan capital in an emergency, and given it was tiny, few villagers actually visited Barcelona in a year.

So the baker daily headed towards the station with high hopes, only to return disappointed.

Meanwhile, nostalgia ate into his soul. Daniel was the rotund Friar Baker no more: his clothes hung looser and looser, longer and longer, his head of hair turned completely white, and a blue circle of bitterness framed his eyes giving him a wild, cadaverous look.

Though Miquelet had little time to devote to him, he noticed his decline and wanted to take him to a doctor. It was hopeless. The sick man was prickly. He had no faith in physicians he didn't know, and worse still, had no desire to be cured. He hated the state he was in, he hated his life, and felt a mysterious longing he could only define as a wish to run, to run far away and hurry along days he found far too drawn out. His volatile moods led him to experience a series of ups and downs from morning to night. He flew into a rage at the sight of a bakery where customers couldn't actually see the oven where the bread was being baked. On other occasions, you might have seen him sweetly entranced, contemplating the birds and flowers sold on La Rambla. If anyone had asked what he could see or why he was delighted, he would certainly have replied that never before had he had the time to watch birds and flowers, and now he loved to do so, though he couldn't say why! Perhaps, unawares, he was discovering a secret connection with spring, the harbinger of summer! Doesn't a man in thrall to a desire everywhere hear the mysterious call of the object of his longing?

The same call no doubt fostered the baker's love of solitude, and even greater fondness for the station area. He wasn't content to go there when the train was about to arrive: every afternoon he strolled around that corner of the city. It was as if the smells from his village reached him along the tracks, scents without which his life wasn't worth living.

One afternoon when his legs carried him past the Convent de les Adoratrices, he came to a spot where the track straightened and continued until it was out of sight, where the rails converged like the tips of a lance disappearing into the distant purple haze. His eyes homed in on that spot, wanting to cross the frontier on the horizon, and drawn by a hidden allure, he sat on the edge of the dip or slope by the track.

The sun sank behind the slopes of Vallvidriera opposite the city; an ashen pall engulfed the houses of Pedralbes, Sarrià, and Sant Gervasi, and the mountain's immense shadow solemnly invaded the plain, as the clouds changed and their streaks of colour blackened.

The dip where the rails ran also darkened by the minute, and the tracks took on a watery gleam in the fading evening light.

Daniel's gaze slid along the rails like the gaze of an exile contemplating a river that finds its source in his distant land. The poor man wept. He couldn't imagine why a path that one day had brought so much pleasure could now depress him so. It demonstrated yet again the truth of the poet: beauty is in the eye of the beholder.

All at once Daniel sprang to his feet and strode towards the hairdressing salon, looking animated, a feeling he'd not had in a long time.

'Thanks be to God you look so happy!' said his son. 'You look like a new man. What's made you so cheerful all of a sudden?'

'I think I've identified my sickness and found my cure. I'm missing the village: I'm going home tomorrow.'

'Have you gone mad, father? How can you live in Barcelona and miss that hamlet in the back of beyond? Don't you remember how you felt when you came here for the first time?'

'All this seemed like heaven then. Now it seems like a graveyard.'

'At least wait till the summer. Do you want for anything here?'

'I want for everything and I want for nothing: try to understand. I'm an old tree that was mistakenly transplanted. If I stay here, I'll die of sadness. Let me go home and don't take it amiss. I'm grateful for everything you've done for me, I love you dearly . . . but I must return home . . . What choice do I have, if I miss it so much . . . ?'

By this stage, Daniel was in tears, and, as he shook his son's hand, he repeated his protestations of gratitude and all the other reasons behind his decision.

Miquelet understood his father's state of mind and accompanied him to the station.

It was too late now. Happiness is like sap, once lost late in life, it can never be recovered. Daniel had lost his forever, and if he thought he could revive it for a time by returning to his land, then he was quickly disabused.

He himself had said as much: he was an old tree that had been transplanted. And when an old tree has been torn from its earth, it's futile trying to replant it back in that same spot: it will never bud again.

Why should I now try to portray that poor baker in his village, deprived of the home and bakery he had so foolishly rented out, losing vigour and colour by the day, staring at the ground, eyes clouded by tears, finding no pleasure in seeing people or chatting to them, joyless in life and with the single hope that he would soon end his suffering in a shroud?

He didn't even last to the summer (which he had so longed to see!): in May, the grass, entangled with wild roses and wisteria, was already enveloping the wrought-iron cross that rose above the grave of the late, lamented Daniel and his wife under the pretty canopy of a pristine spring sky.

Le Petit Journal

TOUS LES JOURS
Le Petit Journal
5 Centimes

SUPPLÉMENT ILLUSTRÉ
Huit pages : CINQ centimes

TOUS LES VENDRE
Le Supplément ill
5 Centimes

atrième Année — SAMEDI 25 NOVEMBRE 1893

LA DYNAMITE EN ESPAGNE

A Brief, Heart-Warming Story of a Madame Bovary Born and Bred in Gràcia, Following our Best Principles and Traditions

Montserrat Roig

When the switch fell I could feel it upon my flesh; when it welled and ridged it was my blood that ran, and I would think with each blow of the switch: Now are you aware of me! Now I am something in your secret and selfish life, who have marked your blood with my own for ever and ever.

William Faulkner, *As I Lay Dying*

In the folds of her lips, her slightly pronounced chin, her wrinkles, her tired eyes, and the white hair of her decrepit majesty, still tall and smiling, Bobby found the full essence of that aristocratic and mercantile Barcelona, popular, proud, and a bit childish, all traces of which were fading.

The widow Xuclà represented all those things, and more. Even more than a man, an old woman who has lived a full life retains the imprint of the past and the sensible permanence of memory. Women have more passive nerve receptors and more receptive souls, so they do not consume themselves nor do they expend all their energy in action as men do. Women are both more covetous and more foresightful. Between the folds of their wrinkled skin, they have the good faith to collect dreams, to gather up adventures, and to preserve there what cannot be seen and can only be sensed: the perfume of history.

Josep-Maria de Sagarra, *Private Life*
(translated by Mary Ann Newman)

Sentimental, frail, and timid temperaments might deem the last noises a human animal emits, before forever leaving a motley, soporific world to be a desperate prayer to return to this life. However, we shouldn't be so sanguine: those fleeting splutters simply indicate the eternal arrest of the bronchial tubes, the last breath, the final rattle.

Mundeta, Mona's grandmother and Ramona's mother, died like that. A brief revival fuelled the family's tenuous illusions: then the last gasp soon ended her futile struggle and put that straight for good. It was a cold, though not icy, January morning and the city was still recovering from its Christmas excesses.

Finally, Tereseta, they have left me alone and I am able to write to you. The parents are at the Liceo; they're performing *Lohengrin* today, an opera by a composer called Wagner. Papa is a great opera lover and he says Wagner is the best composer this century has had. I am lying by the side of my bed with a candle because I don't want the maid to see me. She's a big gossip and always tells Mama what I'm up to.

There is a lot of influenza in Barcelona. Some days over eighty people die. Here in Gràcia we hear the bells toll from time to time and see the cortege process with the last rites, intoning funeral dirges. Papa says the flu was all we needed to add to our headaches.

Grandmother was shrouded in the Carmelite habit of Our Mother of God, that age-old uniform that literary folk from Castile like so much.

I am going to a new school, run by the Mothers of the Sacred Heart, on Torrent de l'Olla, where I spend many a tedious hour staring into the street, where I can see a small strip of sky where clouds come and go. My favourite class is Needlework, because Mother Adelina is in charge. The dullest are French and Catechism.

That garment fully reflects a wish to lend a touch of humility to death's new protagonist, who has just taken her first steps in the role of corpse, allowing her to imagine her accession to the realms of eternity is guaranteed.

While the Father sermonizes, I imagine the clouds passing beyond the big windows.

The dressing ceremony was pure routine. The old lady's skinny, dislocated limbs fall limply on the sheets, and display the imperceptible fatigue of nothingness. The undertakers' staff handle her body gingerly, as if mending vests and darning socks. The definitive touches to her eternal garb were a couple of scapulars placed either side of her body and long, black rosary beads with a wooden cross they tied around her hands that were as thin as hanging threads. The dead woman is now in a fit state to weather the final blasts of the tempest.

That's cotton wool, this one is like the corner of a long rock, the one over there reminds me of the shadow of the Prior's mule, another looks like acacia or mimosa . . .

All these banal, petty details, hardly striking enough to be the stuff of imagination, will serve to enlighten the reader as to the extraordinary vulgarity of Mundeta Jover i Almirall's demise. Already beginning to betray the simple, unchanging features of the everyday nature of death, the old lady was positioned unglamorously in the coffin. Everybody knows that undertakers have a tunnel vision of history: one, two, three, four candles; two level with her shoulders and two next to her feet illuminated the deceased's unshakeable serenity. The candles brushing against her lower extremities, that almost touched the door step, magnified the shadows from the nearby wall from time to time.

I am embroidering the loveliest images. I'll send you one as a memento. I have created a child Jesus dragging a very large cross on one and it is obviously too heavy because he is sweating profusely.

The family lamentations were relatively subdued. Rhythmically they were in perfect harmony with the situation. Several neighbours under twenty, the kind whose loving tenderness has yet to give way to the prickliness inspired by first contact with the flesh, halted in front of the coffin and pondered on the duration of human frailty.

He is sweating little drops of blood I have sewn with red silk thread. He wears a crown of thorns, that makes me feel very sad, because I think it must hurt awfully, but Mother Teresa says that best suits him. His tiny feet are resting on a pink cloud, and he is clad in a golden garment with sky-blue furbelows gathered in folds.

Mundeta Jover i Almirall was lamented, remembered, and forgotten, as the rules dictated by our strict domestic moral code require. In any case, it is well known that our ancient moral code, that has been so well preserved, is not very different from those manufactured according to European norms. The tears shed by humanity over the years, to its total satisfaction, come to create, in their purity, a framework for sorrow within the best classical sense of the golden mean. However, if Mundeta provoked the necessary tears to uphold our hallowed traditions, God knows, a sense of loss joined the flow too.

I don't know if I told you that when I came back from Siurana, Papa gave me the prettiest doll by the name of *Grazielle*. She's wearing a light green dress with a silk lace collar. She has plaited fair hair, and moves her legs up and down. She is very tall, almost like an actual girl, and can open and close her eyes.

I sing to her:

> Ma poupée est la plus gentille
> de celles qu'on voit ici-bas,
> j'adore ma petite fille,
> elle m'aime, et ne pleure pas!*

Two funeral wreaths lie at the foot of the coffin. In the best of the worst Barcelonan taste, they are adorned with purple ribbons graced with saccharine literary phrases that knowingly exhibit the refined sensibility of our distant relatives. Philosophical disquisitions on death, pensive

* 'My doll is the loveliest / of all you see down here / I love my little girl / she loves me, and doesn't cry!'

words on the passage of time, to the point of no return. (Here, the author grants herself licence to suggest more garish, gaudier colours for those wreaths: possibly red and yellow; thus demonstrating our love of contrasts, which, into the bargain, would be decently patriotic.)

Dear Tereseta. Do you know what it means to get up early one morning, gaze into the sky and find it bluer and brighter than on any previous day, to intuit, across workaday Barcelona, the sea caressing and cuddling the sand, and dream of acacia leaves rustling on La Rambla as they flutter to the rhythm of a breeze coming from the east?

And if I were to add that I feel my blood simmering and bubbling within me to the extent that my ears turn a bright red! I would love to proclaim my happiness from the balcony, but that is hardly becoming for a young lady . . .

Because, can you imagine, tonight I shall make my debut at the Liceo? Which means that the adult world, once so unattainable, will now finally become *my* world. Because, as Mama says, a visit to the Liceo means you meet the important people of Barcelona, and catch up on the latest French fashions, behave more elegantly, and show off the finery of a real lady, like Mama, and use the same perfumes as her, the same jewels, hats, and even silk stockings from Paris.

Today the new season is launched with Rossini's *William Tell*; it's not been performed in Barcelona for seven years.

Initially, Papa moaned, because he says Rossini is more light opera than anything else and that he cuts a sad figure by the side of Wagner. But Mama, who's good at soft-soaping him, persuaded him to rent a box. We will go with Clara and Maria Jordana. Climent the widow will come too—she calls herself a widow, but the Rieras' maid told me her husband ran off to Havana with a French chorus girl; this widow wants to introduce us to her nephew who has just arrived from Madrid. Tereseta, I must leave you, Mama has been calling me for some time. I've still to try on my shoes and gloves for this evening.

Primitive peoples were right to celebrate the joy of death with feasts and parties: the first enlightened civilizations demonstrated that inebriation is the best dirge.

The Liceo was packed. Before we went in, we saw a big crowd gathering in front of the main entrance, desperate to get an unimpeded view of the spectacle in the street. Some—I suppose they were students—wanted tickets for the fourth and fifth floors, and others—children and florists—simply huddled together entranced by the carriages and diligences stopping there. Everybody was jammed into the top of Carrer Sant Pau, and the police, who wore white plumes on their helmets, were struggling to contain the heaving mass. Papa was so elegant he was totally adorable. For a second I dreamt I was his partner and that he was accompanying me to protect me from some strange peril. Naturally, it was a daydream, but I really imagined it was true. Papa wore the most immaculate evening attire, a white shirt-front, starched like a breastplate, a four-inch high collar and a long black silk tie. Mama was exquisite too, as I've often told you, her brown hair shines with copper glints . . . It was all so sumptuous, so palatial I couldn't get over it. The ladies' jewels sparkled in the boxes, and their dresses shimmered when they shook their fans. The gentlemen seemed as stiff as cardboard—some, I confess, looking like turkey-cocks—and hovered gallantly among the ladies.

The lights went out and, apart from the whispering in the boxes, the theatre assumed the degree of silence and respect that the work merited. A wave of perfume occasionally wafted our way—we were in the dress circle—and almost made us gulp. I felt ecstatic to be part of that realm of wealth, happiness, and luxury!

On the other hand, in our Eixample, the prayers, laments, and platitudes, even the mourning, are overwhelmingly drab. Like the purple curtains we made with long yellowish hems—a colour bequeathed by history—with the crimson carpets and rugs adding to their inevitable tawdriness. That's how it is and there's nothing one can do.

However, we should leave this subtle, minute survey of our lack of extravagance for another time.

The funeral was correct down to the tiniest detail: absolutely *comme il faut*. The whole host of the pillars of society were in attendance, as is the case with every Barcelona family of high standing, and even posher. Hats, shawls, or headscarves—according to age and status—paraded by with vice-regal restraint as part of the cortege. Hints of smiles, sideways glances, brief gestures, bland greetings, furtive pats, looks that said what a lovely-gift-from-God and how-grown-up-she-is lent a cheerful, exhilarating tone to the occasion. The deceased lay in her coffin, far from almost anyone's thoughts, except, perhaps, for Ramona and her daughter, Mundeta.

All of a sudden—it was the middle of the second act—a bang resonated, like a pistol shot. Somebody screamed and the stalls were enveloped by a cloud of thick, bluish smoke that began to rise up to the higher floors.

For the others, the start of the ceremony, when the ravages of death were re-affirmed, reinforced their unique sweetly voluptuous pleasure at the way they controlled the universe. What bliss those mean, corroded spirits experienced, as they did—*gratias ad Dominem*—their belief in life's ineluctable progression towards the mystery of death!

My memories are confused, but I think I remember Mama trying to take my arm and say something or other about a second explosion and, then, I got lost among the people running towards the exits where a vast crowd had gathered. The ottomans in the restrooms were filling up with the wounded who were crying out—I later discovered some were dying—and I remember ending up in the arms of Francisco Ventura, widow Clement's nephew, who told me that anarchists had caused the explosion.*

I am sitting by our fireside, with Lola, our seamstress. She lives on Carrer Mercaders and comes up three times a week. She told me over thirty died and that the police have caught the culprits. A second bomb fell on the skirt of a lady who had been killed by the blast from the first.

I can hear Papa saying this government is entirely to blame and that he can't believe that the attempt on the life of General Martínez Campos wasn't sufficient warning.

I feel very, very numb. I can't tell you anymore. Just look how my first visit to the Liceo ended.

The religious service, including communion and sermon (in their abbreviated versions), didn't go on for too long. The old, flat-footed priest and his younger assistant added the last brushstrokes to ensure it was a fine spectacle and guaranteed a passport to the next world. The young chaplain got the Gospel all mixed up, changed tenses, verses, and words and produced a stew that was so incoherent it brought light relief to the gloom of the moment.

I am to marry and I can tell you I barely know him. On first impression he seemed a good person; perhaps rather

* The bomb was thrown into the stalls by anarchist Santiago Salvador on 7 November 1893.

lacking in verve, and a sedate, unsociable fellow. He dresses most handsomely but sometimes I would like to glimpse a touch of melancholy in his expression, of the kind you find in romantic souls.

Les Corts cemetery is one of the smallest, best constructed in Barcelona. Because, as Aunty Sista—Patrícia Miralpeix's cousin—says, it is 'lots of fun, and one has wonderful walks there when the sun shines.'

I am ambitious and don't hold my future husband in high enough regard, which cannot be a good thing: he is a good-looking, polite, refined gentleman, and his expression is both charming and energetic. I couldn't hope for anyone better. I sometimes wonder whether I'm one of those individuals who are never happy with their fate. The kind that is always seeking other worlds to experience beyond the one that's been allotted.

It is located in the residential district in west Barcelona, between Sarrià and Pedralbes, and two squares: Pope Pius XII and Queen Maria Cristina (I will leave it to the reader to make the necessary comparisons). Beyond them, the Maternity Hospital and Mental Institute open the way to that majestic sanctuary of the Catalan masses: Barça's Estadi Nou.

He paid the occasional visit, especially when Papa was there, and adopted a stiff, cardboard stance that meant he seemed less gracious and elegant, and, for my taste, I then found him to be far too vulgar.

The house of the dead looks northwards. From the entrance, the streets and side streets supplied fine panoramic views, the most pleasant of aromas, and a clean, refined, exquisite layout. Visitors who had the good fortune (or misfortune, depending on how you see it) to enter there alive and were possessed by a sensibility suited to contemplative meditation, could stroll and be suffused by that silent spectacle *à la recherche du temps perdu*, and when finished, depart with their minds completely transformed.

I write to you from Paris, capital of the world and city of lights. We arrived three days ago, and I am taking advantage of a moment's relaxation in our hotel room to write—just imagine, we have a bathroom for our sole use! No need for me to tell you about our wedding: you can imagine it all. I have become Francisco Ventura's 'joy', 'bliss', and 'queen', in other words, Senyora Ventura. While straightening out some wrinkles in the eiderdown, I will read Francisco's latest poem:

I was born to love you alone,
Ramona within my heart,
and love you more than is possible
and my love is so sensitive,
so pure, so vivid, so beautiful
that I want to live eternally
burying any moment that is sorrowful
in the allure of your seductive charms.
Your adoring Francisco.

So there you have it, not a day passes when I don't find a sample of his amorous effusions in a dress pocket or by my knife and fork on the dining-room table. However, if at first I found that captivating, now it *irritates* me. I know full well I have to respond in some way.

It goes without saying that Paris induces a mad flurry of different emotions. But I'm terrified that one day I will leave this city—that I find so exciting—without exploring it in any depth. I will have passed through like a visitor. Dark, sinister side streets I glimpse from the carriage, or resplendently frivolous ladies, or marvellously bohemian artists will only leave me with a strange feeling of experiences I shall never enjoy. I've not breathed the gaiety of Paris, I've not seen anything exotic, I've caught nothing in the atmosphere—as romantic novels describe—no sudden glance, no incipient smile, no emotion to distinguish the air of Paris from the air of Barcelona. And fully aware that my stay here will be *the* journey of my life, I don't want to miss a single leaf in the Bois de Boulogne or Vincennes, or a single streetlight in Pigalle or cobblestone in Montmartre.

A twilight stroll through the cemetery in spring or autumn, when daylight dims and the sun slips between rooftops, and the newly grown or half-golden leaves do not rustle . . . A stroll, we would say, that should be noted in the 'diary of good intentions' of any self-respecting citizen of Barcelona.

Deep in the central gardens, past a short avenue, you come to a collection of pantheons. Apart from the occasional mausoleum that solidly represents the last traces of an aristocratic Barcelona, the pantheons are arranged in a circle and occupy the whole of the central zone.

Nevertheless, neither the gardens, columns, lakes, and salons of Versailles, nor the imposing, majestic Louvre, not the heavenly or hellish cabarets, nor the delightful attractions of the dogs' cemetery, will ever make me forget my Rambla, our port and sea.

Their disposition obeys the principles of comfort and ease so rooted in tradition, and gathers in a single precinct the entire remnants of our family memories.

In this way, our families are forever united after they pass away, with a cohesion that is indestructible and metaphysically sealed against all external malevolence.

A gentleman visited the other day, I think he works for the Hispano-Colonial Bank and he told me that what's happening in Cuba is only because they'd not sent anyone who knew how to beat the living daylights out of the rebels. Everyone is talking about how the last outposts of the Spanish regiments have been destroyed in Santiago de Cuba and Cavite. Nevertheless, everyone is full of hope. I can see that people in the street are quite euphoric, and the fact is, if news comes, it can only mean that the war is ending, and for the good of Spain.*

* Spain lost its colony, Cuba, in the 1898 war against the United States.

Yesterday morning, my dear Tereseta, they inaugurated the electric tramline in Gràcia. By the Virgin Mary, there was such a commotion! Everywhere was garlanded with all kinds of flowers, and the pillars of our society were contented, smiling, and more in control than ever. Compared to the previous mule-driven tram, this one moves like a shooting star. Some of my lady friends are afraid to climb on board; a rumour abounds from Italy that people who tread on the rail immediately die. You know, nonsense concocted by country bumpkins. The electric current doesn't pass through the rail, but the overhead cable! But what can one do? Some people are so ignorant! Dolores, the embroiderer, who has a half-loony sister, had a set-to with the authorities. It turns out that this woman, one of the nosiest in Gràcia, wanted to be the first into the tram. What a calamity! She shoved her way through the police until she was right in the middle of the tram; it was a real struggle to remove her! The wife of the mayor, by the name of Pauleta Forns, and a friend of mine, was truly indignant: 'What is that wretch doing, *madre mía*, how dare she?'

When she was dragged out, fuming, her hair dishevelled, she still had the cheek to give herself the airs of a duchess.

The apparent indissolubility of human bonding, wrought so painstakingly, will continue unchanged on its way to the next life thanks to this architecture. The pantheons have so many features and adornments, filigree, the early Byzantine-Gothic-Baroque twirls and accompanying additions are in keeping with the pantheons' grandeur and volume. The most common are a middling size, the height of a wood cabin, little turreted spires: they are abodes for pretentious dreamers, a little shop-owner from Santa Maria del Mar, or Carrers Canvis, Agullers, Tamborets, or any of the Calls, higher up the city. They rejoice in massive slabs of granite with an off-white patina, and come accompanied by literary gems fashioned by grey family minds and flecked with vegetarian or metaphorical insights. The most frequent trait of these minds is the inability to draw with minimal precision and objectivity a portrait that would humanly and spiritually characterize their deceased.

We celebrated my birthday yesterday. I am now twenty-three. And still childless. I've no wish to philosophize, and will just tell you what we did. Francisco took me out to lunch at Casa Justin, where for five *pessetes* you eat as if you were in paradise. First course, delicious macaroni à la Languedoc, followed by a rabbit I imagine was wild with a Catalan *romesco* sauce. I drank lots of wine and champagne. You can imagine how the festivities ended. Even though Francisco and I, because of that phantom child who never comes, barely dare look at each other when we're in bed. When he is asleep and I can hear him snoring by my side, because, he snores, you know, I think about our lives and really don't know what to conclude. I feel he is a stranger . . . ay, but I don't know why I am telling you this.

Yesterday, after lunch, he gave me earrings where two huge rubies nestled. He also brought a poem:

> Love and reverence
> I promised when I met you,
> and so you are convinced
> I will love you to the end of existence.
> Ramona deep in my heart,
> of all things the finest present,
> with your sweet presence
> you fill the flower's absence.
> Your love, that adores you.

Last Sunday, we went for a stroll and ended up at the Café del Siglo XX, in Plaça de Catalunya. Everybody calls it 'The Aviary'. We listened to music for a while because it's a suntrap. I love to smell the scent from the oleanders and acacias coming from La Rambla, as I listen to the waltz of *The Hundred Maidens*. And it is so quiet! I have to confess I sometimes find peaceful Barcelona to be rather tiresome, and would like lots of things to be happening. But what can one do? Apart from the occasional anarchist attack, that are less and less frequent, thanks be to God, Barcelona only offers us balm. It's a pretty, cheerful city; we have the sea and La Rambla.

Side paths ascend, narrowing all the time, to the cemetery's gloomy, shadowy zones. It's the farthest spot from the scents from the central grove of trees.

We are at the turn of the century. We have changed eight to nine and almost not noticed. It feels most peculiar to have a hundred years behind one.

Francisco spent the whole of yesterday afternoon arguing with Sr Domingo, a very *catalanero* moneylender who's a member of Unió Regionalista, about whether the new century begins in 1900 or 1901. Francisco is one of those men who, once he gets an idea into his head, defends it as stubbornly as a mule, and nobody will budge him. Sr Domingo reached the conclusion that, if the century begins in 1901, then 1900 doesn't exist. The things people find to argue about!

We have moved from Gràcia. We have gone to a flat on Carrer Còrsega between Passeig de Gràcia and Claris. Such heavenly sunlight comes in from the balcony! Our building has three floors and we're on the first. All four balconies look over the street, and I've filled them with carnations, geraniums, hydrangeas, morning glory . . . a lark, two canaries, and a green parakeet who calls out: 'Come here, Ramona.' There are two shops at street level, either side of the main entrance. Our house, as I think I have already indicated, is a suntrap, and I could spend the whole day idling on the balcony. I would be distracted observing how people walk by, how they talk, how they stop and chat to shopkeepers . . . I would lay bets as to who is riding in carriages, who is alighting from trams . . .

The wall around the inside of the cemetery is a mass of niches. The concave spaces are all the same, same area, exact sizes and colours. Built from limestone with a uniformly sepulchral tone, the only variant is an outside wall shutting off the abode of the dead. Some niches have only a smooth, flat, white stone that is completely bare. Others seem to have opted for the most extravagant ornamentation imaginable, that is even uglier than the curlicues on the pantheons, because size is never in proportion to the decorative excess. Here, the walls are limited by space and covered with reliefs in the broadest range of floral shapes that all remind one of lilies. Small vases of flowers, placed between glass and stone, often exude an exuberant exotic artificiality, and signal the colossal meanness of Barcelona's middle classes who shun their pasts as fin-de-siècle artisans. Sometimes, nevertheless, a small flower, a precise word, the shadow of a memory, evokes the enigmatic melancholy of the void.

Yesterday Pauleta Forns repaid a visit I made to her a week ago. She wore that yellow hat to cover her head. She thinks nobody knows she is bald. As ever, she is her usual impertinent self and her vulgar owlish eyes scrutinize the furnishing in our Turkish room where I keep my childhood porcelain dolls. She is envious. But hides that so well, she is just like an actress from the Diorama Theatre. Her foolish chatter drives me crazy. I think she sensed something the other day:

'Am I in the way, dear?'

'No, I'm sorry. I got out of bed with a migraine and feel rather frail.'

Then she smiled rudely. She is a lucky lady and always gets it right. She never stops talking to me about her 'fortunate marriage', how 'her' Carlus is the kindest, loveliest man God ever placed on this earth, or whether Merceditas, poor dear, is a victim of her husband, or Elvira, another unhappy soul, has made a bad marriage to that pathetic wretch, how she and 'her' Carlus are thinking of visiting Paris in the spring . . .

And Carlus is simply a scarecrow who struts around as if he were a gentleman. I know he has lodged a chorus girl in a flat.

They buried Grandmother Ramona in one of those concave sepulchral spaces; the coffin fitted perfectly, next to Francisco, the creator of Mundeta Jover's celestial heaven.

I gave birth to a girl four months ago. We called her Ramona. Francisco insisted it's a lovely name, he's so stubborn. I think it sound rustic, but what one can do! I must confess I would have preferred a boy. At least a man is free and does what he wants.

The niche was in the main wall, a location parallel to more luxurious, exemplary resting places. Oriented seawards, the corpse, if it so wishes, can enjoy a beautiful view. The height of these lower niches doesn't reach the nose level of a person of average height, which helps root the deceased in the earth. When it was time to forever seal the wall that would separate Ramona from the world of the living, someone threw in a small carnation, a symbol perhaps, for those who remembered, of the final farewell.

All theatres have been closed as a result of the shambles of Setmana Tràgica—which is what they call the disastrous days in July.* Now they are gradually reopening. Yesterday I went to see *Don Gonçal or the Lizard's Prize.*

We sometimes lunch at the Maison Dorée or the Café Suís. I prefer the Maison Dorée; it is *so* elegant and stylish. It reminds me of Paris, with its Versailles touches and sumptuous illumination. I simply adore their Italian macaroni perfumed with truffles. They say they are the composer Rossini's favourite dish in Paris.

For the first time we saw Francisca Màrquez perform; Raquel Meller is her pseudonym. As she is from Aragon, I don't think she will go very far. Francisco prefers this Raquel to the Fornarina woman. I find her rather common, though she could hardly be as cheap and flirtatious

* Violent confrontations between the army and the working class in Barcelona in the last week of July 1909.

as Bella Chelito. Years ago I would never have imagined Francisco would become obsessed by music-hall songs. He has even forgotten who Wagner is.

One must return from the cemetery slowly, very slowly. Carrer de les Corts, Carrer d'Europa, Carrer de Joan Güell . . . Re-entry into the world of the living, into this material, real, contingent world, can turn one's principles upside down. First, one must leave through the front gate, the old door that's now the entrance for cars, and observe the change in atmosphere with the eye of someone who knows he will never return there. Such an impassive, confident attitude infuses spirits who desire peace, work, and good health with the immense, extraordinary conformity of the middle way.

> *And, thus, you have left this world of the living forever: you have entered the abode of those who will never return; who knows if you savoured the bliss of death in your solitude. I would like your abyss to be pitch-black, eternally black, and for you never to be aware of how you were deceived. Those who preceded you in life distorted your possible lucidity. Your contemporaries undermined your vitality, your grandeur and plunged you into the facile morass of their own tawdry principles. Those who succeeded you didn't know how to understand you and believed you, otherwise they weren't far wrong, and also stood for the mystical delirium that had sustained the morality of the strong.*

All in all they dictated norms that were to direct your life along the narrow, rocky paths of unawareness.

Because you didn't know any of all that, because you passed through this world silently, imperceptibly, with the lightness of those who speak to themselves, I would like your mortal slumber to be compact, dense, without shadows of disillusion and suffering.

And now, from a Barcelona that is beginning to lose even its dethroned queen's nostalgia, I shall try to create for you the perfume of history.

Ramon from Montjuic

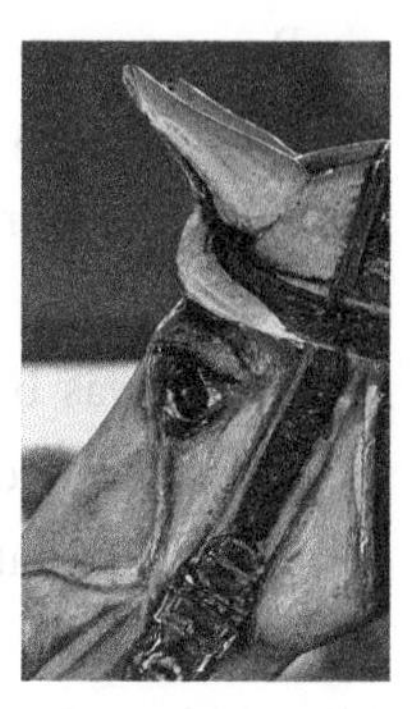

Josep Pla

The tragic death of my friend Ramon, a denizen of the northern skirts of Montjuic—the one that touches Poble-sec—saddened me and reminded me of a past era in my life. Deceased Ramon owned a small, ramshackle amusement park consisting of a roundabout and a booth with a shooting range. The park opened in summer and in winter the owner used his magical powers to transform the park into an afternoon dance hall.

The whole lot occupied the shadowy depths of an orchard on a Poble-sec street that climbed up the mountain. You had to cross a sprawling, noisy, boisterous neighbourhood to reach it.

Ramon was a Sunday friend. In winter, I'd almost always go to his place after Sunday lunch. We'd survived six days of university constraint, and could be light-headed for a few hours: it was a true escape. At that time of day Poble-sec was bathed in large expanses of warm, sunny silence perfumed by the bittersweet smell of oranges past their prime. That intense, still tranquillity was constantly under assault from the distant cries of a gang of squabbling kids and the dull rumble from taverns full of guitars twanging monotonously. As you walked by, you'd spot the musician by a marble-topped table, twisted around, one leg crossed over another, displaying a red sock, a cigarette behind his ear, a forelock of hair, twirled like a rolled wafer over his temples, surrounded by a large circle of wet, gaping mouths.

I remember, as if it were today, the precentor's voice of an old, tall, bearded blind man who walked around Poble-sec singing the ballad of the shipwreck of the *Valbanera*. Locals crowded onto their balconies to listen: women in their petticoats, men in their yellow overalls. When the blind man walked past taverns, he trod on peanut shells, and, as he clearly hated the noise, he'd hop quickly over them like a clumsy bird. In the tavern doorway there was always a young worker, an oblique figure, in an ironed blue suit, the band of his peaked cap on the slant, a fag-end on his lips, a carnation in his ear, swaggering and silent, a hint of roosterish cruelty on his lips. Girls from Castile and Aragon also walked arm in arm, a pink-apple, mother-of-pearl glow on their cheeks, their hair wet, wavy, and combed flat. These girls sometimes gave a helping hand to small, weary, snub-nosed soldiers who chomped on orange peel and peanut shells.

There were a lot of the war-wounded, crippled, maimed, and poor, and occasionally they formed a kind of barricade with their walking sticks, twisted limbs, wooden legs, crutches, and the other tools of the trade this hapless crew possessed.

After crossing this neighbourhood, I took the road to the castle. I turned down a track that followed the glacis, sat down for a while to gaze at the sky, the wintry Barcelona sky, which is beautiful, especially on windy days—a sky where white clumps of cloud scudded over warm blues, faded greens, and crimson haze—and later, with a sprig of thyme between my lips, hands in pockets, my feelings and thoughts wandering vaguely, I'd amble down the path to that rudimentary park, where a pompous municipal building stood among foliage, reach the skirts of the mountain and go to take a look at the late-lamented Ramon's afternoon dance.

I did so with trepidation because the fug inside made me feel dizzy and the dim lights kept flickering. When my eyes adapted, in the centre of that shabby marquee I could discern a kiosk made from four staves supporting a platform surrounded by chicken wire. Perched inside that cage, in a sea of smoke and dust, were the murky figures of three musicians clinging to their instruments as if they were lifebuoys. The gaslight reflected in dull, vaguely melancholy fashion on the gilded metal of a flugelhorn. In the background, you could see the merry-go-round under wraps in the late evening gloom. Between that grandiose hulk and the marquee's canvas walls a large slit allowed you a glimpse of the starry night.

When the musicians weren't playing, there was a muffled hubbub of noise in the marquee. Occasionally a girl screamed in that Spanish chocolate-hued circle of hustle and bustle as if she'd just lost a tooth. Children played chase between the legs of dancers and sometimes three or four rolled in a ball across the floor. There was always a mother sitting on a chair suckling a child. The wan, lined complexions of these mothers, in that light, made me think of Sisley's paintings, though I'm not sure why.

Ramon always carried a stick he used to adjust the gas lamps and remove grease. He slithered around like an eel, was everywhere, shouted at the musicians, kept an eye on the ticket office, sorted out problems, moved on people jamming the entrance, ejected bad payers and troublemakers.

Rather than simply sound forth, the music groaned and roared. It was bodily driven, pure explosions from the lungs that hit you in the guts. When it started up, a huge, rowdy, garish mass of humanity swirled around the cage, swelling, changing shape. On bank holidays the plume on some soldier's tin helmet would stick out above people's heads, a hussar's helmet floating over the polkas and mazurkas. Dust turned the gaslights red, the haze was granulated, speckled with droplets of greyish pus.

Ramon was a small, lean, bald man with thick, bushy eyebrows. He wore an ironed rubber collar and celluloid cuffs; his voice was gravelly and he drawled like a superannuated comedian. It was obvious he longed to be a bohemian artist, because he let the nail on his little finger grow, made outlandish statements, and had a tendency to dress like a dandy: he wore, for example, a pale turtle-coloured fancy waistcoat and wielded a gnarled wooden walking stick. This vein in Ramon's spiritual life found expression in his passion to go rod-fishing on the breakwater, a thing he loved to do, even though he was a third-rate fisherman.

Ramon was a human beanpole who concealed huge sloth behind a façade of decency. Essentially he was what good writers call a misunderstood man. He took an interest in anything out of the ordinary. He felt that working, that is, organizing a dance, on a day when everybody else had a day off, was proof of his superiority.

Ramon lived on the merry-go-round. His kitchen was at the top. His pantry was in the belly of one of the papier-mâché horses that pranced up and down. He hung his clothes on the trumpets played by the carousel organ's nymphs. He welcomed people sitting on his rose-garlanded portable chair—the chair children's mothers used on the merry-go-round. He kept a stack of four small shabby, brown-painted boxes, four old shoes, faded clothes, and long, extravagant fishing rods in the circular hollow between the central column and revolving round-about. When he walked through the Barceloneta with his rods, he hoped to create a big stir.

The most original touch was his bedroom. Ramon would hoist himself into the bellows of his carousel's organ. The bellows were connected to the carrousel by a mesh and a pulley. When the merry-go-round went around, the bellows swelled and deflated. When it was full of wind, the bellows looked like a truncated pyramid, a kind of frog's mouth with a leather-covered iron frame that folded when deflated. The bellows were set horizontally behind the frieze of nymphs and dancers who lifted gilt trumpets to their lips and whose swollen cheeks pretended to puff when the nasal-toned organ played.

I remember telling Ramon one day that it was dangerous to sleep in that lair.

'One day, the carousel will start up for some reason and the bellows will compress and you will be squashed to death. Luckily, however,' I added with a laugh, 'while you're being ironed as flat as a pair of trousers, the nymphs' trumpets will blast out a fanfare and the dancers will raise a leg.'

'It will be a death with a charm of its own,' he retorted in that childishly vain tone artists adopt when vaunting their peculiar eccentricities, and scratched his wrinkled forehead and bushy eyebrows with the long yellow nail of his little finger.

When I heard that Ramon had died, I went to the amusement park. I entered the orchard. Not a living soul was to be seen. The shooting range was shut up and the carrousel covered over. I was about to leave when I saw a woman with a sack of paper over her shoulder and an orange in one hand.

'They buried him yesterday,' she said. 'They found him dead inside the bellows.'

'Why did he die?'

'Nobody knows. The day before yesterday he went to the breakwater with his fishing rods and today he is pushing up the daisies.'

'Do you live around here?' I asked.

'Yes, why? You're not a policeman, are you?'

'Did the neighbours hear the roundabout's trumpets blast out a fanfare the night he died?'

'I think I heard someone say something of the sort... You are a policeman, aren't you?'

A slight pause. Then: 'Did Sr. Ramon have many enemies?'

'I don't know, but who would!'

'Perhaps someone from the breakwater, you know?' I retorted, to spin out the conversation.

'He was a good man, but a dead loss,' she muttered incoherently. 'You know, they didn't find a scrap of paper in his storage...'

'You collect paper in the street, right?' I asked, without looking up.

'Yes, senyor, why?'

Another short pause. I poked the ground with my thin, gnarled stick, using its point to dig out a clean white pebble.

'Did anyone go to his funeral?' I asked, blankly.

The woman stared at me, her face shook, and she couldn't stifle her laughter. Then she began peeling her orange.

I looked at her, rather at a loss. I realized I had committed a gaffe. What a peculiar question! I thought of the last funeral I'd heard about, which had been packed out. I said: 'I'm sorry. Enjoy your orange.'

'Thank you!' replied the woman, keeping her eyes on her orange.

Then I went out into the street and walked slowly away.

Blitz on Barcelona

C. A. Jordana

Clair de lune

Clair de lune. Bright, liquid notes. Quicksilverly slipping and slithering. Classical music. Music for a rendezvous, for a movie. The loving couple sing of their passion. A clichéd sheaf of beams spotlights them. The horrible husband surprises them. Unique in this world, he and she emerge in the moonlight to plot. Melancholy, floods of feeling. Deliquescent hearts. Novels, novels, novels.

Nonetheless, moonlight, you are so beautiful and splendid! Your fragile melancholy is so powerful! The stars melt. Spellbound and dizzy, the night pales. White night, so intense and so sweet. Silver dust slanting down covers the street in a luminous haze. Pianos trill from open balconies.

Oh Selene, don't bring anything else tonight! It's all so perfect: silver in the gentle air, musical notes flowing, melancholy filling our hearts. Let us be true romantics, like your sweet face. Sweet. Maybe. A bit comic too, but comedy that doesn't lead to laughs. Curious. Nosey. You lift the veil from the city. You look and show. You took a good peep at the weather forecast.

We'll have unpleasant visitors, that's clear. Sirens and whistles herald them already. Houses suddenly go blind. Ill-omened vibrations in the air. The silver airways thicken with sheaves of white light dispatched by a world on alert.

They have come, trusting in a moon that reveals the city to them, but doesn't show them to the city. Only their noise betrays them, and eyes and searchlights duly scrutinize the sky. No! They are there. Luminously exposed. Friendly beams converge, hold them there, apparently carry them on a tray of light. Their undoubted haste isn't evident. They seem to advance calmly, a swarm of wasps, with shiny wings extended.

You would think it was so tranquil up above! Human heads and hearts soar upwards in aeroplanes. Navigating over a city bathed in clean, sweet moonlight, you should enjoy only elevated thoughts. At a thousand metres, all family quarrels should be forgotten; at two thousand, political passion, national rancour, desire to destroy should evaporate. Divine serenity, indulgent at the very least towards those below, should be an aviator's natural attribute.

But the gods are cruel. Haughty indifference allows them to strike in good cheer. Serene heights only strip their cruelty of any pretext to the moral high ground. Cruel and mean. Guilty angst. Serenity is only apparent, a game distance plays on the eye. They swoop swiftly, desperate to shed the stubborn sheaves of light and dodge the flight of avenging missiles. The city recognizes them, holds them, surrounds them with its fire. Perhaps one has already paid the price? Lagging behind, it disappears in the moonlight. But the charge renews, bitterly flays the air; it bursts into flames on the back of the mountain. The whole city shakes from the explosions.

They have fled. Free from all danger, they can now regain the serene heights, enjoying the divine ease of those who are above all human suffering. Can they really? They have taken the basest earthly passions to those altitudes, and drawn on them on their flights like precious ballast. Can they now recover their serenity? More likely, vile, feverish glee. They count their blasts of fire; they calculate the *targets* hit; they weigh up the *impact on morale*.

Clair de lune. Bright, liquid notes. The night music, interrupted by explosions, now sounds a warm, horrifying note. Ambulance bells ring out sweetly, count the dead and the wounded, accompany the moans and the sighs along the city's streets. Military targets and impact on morale in the living flesh of destroyed homes and tortured bodies! But the luminous brightness sees nothing, wants to know nothing. Is it cruel? Or simply senseless? It would prefer to recast its spell. Sweetness, melancholy, deliquescent bodies. But sorrow is stronger. Its light is fiercer and can fire a city's heart. Oh Selene, romantic myth, liquid music, silver threads, lantern for enemy planes! You can, if you so wish, offer your light against us. That won't stop us doing what we have to do.

(12 July 1938)

* * *

The Hospital

'Aeroplanes. Ten fascist two-engine have bombed the city of... Much of the civilian population has been hit.'

A brief, spare item of news. You've heard it from all over the world, considered it for a second—so brief and spare—and then relegated it to some cranny of the mind. More urgent matters—lunch, cold supper, hot jazz, courting, Mr Chamberlain's prattle—demand the world's attention. That bit of news was parked well out of sight. Though it can't be entirely put to rest. It sprouts, goads with painful thorns: anxiety blossoms—oh, hardly any, for a moment—gathers and converges—a flurry of fleeting thoughts—on that hospital.

A hospital ward. Surrounded by the bustle and white coats of his assistants, the doctor walks on, beds slipping past on either side with their wounded. The stark glare from the windows comes tinged with an undefinable smell—disinfectants, sweat of distress, suffering flesh, urine, fumes from spirit. A lifted sheet reveals a heavily bandaged thigh that's almost disappeared. A deft hand empties half a bottle of Dakin into the tube sticking out from the bandages. The patient groans: 'I'll never get better.' 'Yes, you will, love: all that will grow back,' says a young voice routinely, walking by. 'And what about you?' A woman in her twenties is in the next bed. When they speak to her, she blushes thinking about the dampness she cannot stop. A piece of shrapnel pierced her from behind, shred tissue, dodged bones, reached the bladder. The young woman thus lost control. Now she can't stop apologizing to the extremely young nurse—a lad who is almost a child. 'I didn't do that before,' she mumbles, 'I never wet the bed.' 'Course you didn't, love,' says the young aide, amused, deftly undoing bandages with his boyish hands. He thinks these heart-wrenching excuses are comically superfluous.

But everyone has gone quiet. Even the blind woman quarrelling with the deaf girl in the nearest bed. Accompanied by an experienced, efficient nurse, the doctor now stops opposite half a burning face that stands out against the pillow. The sheet—a protective tent against sight of the devastation—is pulled up to the face, as far as the temples, and one eye looks out—in a delirious stare—and challenges the world. Pulled from the rubble after a bombing raid, it turned out that the youth had been left with half a face. Wounded, hospitalized and in pain, he now thinks, in agony, eye glaring: 'I look horrific. I always will.' And all goes silent for a moment.

But the visit resumes, the voices—rapid exchanges, precise instructions—start turning and shifting again, while fingers clean, bandage and smiles try to encourage. Tracking the voices, following deep surges of pain, we go to the operating room. Bright lights, gleaming, hard lines, asepsis. The doctor, standing, spotlessly white, and the patient, prostrate, a feverish red. The shattered foot must be cleaned, scraped, hewn. The whole ankle is missing, an absence reflected higher up in the young face that's so pathetically contorted. Ends of tendons stick out from blood-stained rags. Bottles and tools are ready. Nimble hands as well. But first the injured girl must be taken into a world of silence. The gas of the anaesthetic softens her face, the metal clamp's fixed. The drops of ether fall. Suffer, suffer, suffer! The patient writhes. She must be choked by the anaesthetic so as not to suffer in the operation. Then back into the world to suffer some more . . .

From the report by Mr Peter Searcher and M. Paul de la Trouvaille: 'The last bombing raid on the city of . . . seems to have purely targeted the civilian population. True enough, there is a shoe factory next to one of the places where bombs were dropped, and shoes are often considered to be good missiles in many a fight. It doesn't fall within our remit to determine in this report whether shoes are an item to be listed in this particular case as worthy of defining a military target. Our opinion is that the bombing raid wasn't aimed at those shoes, taking into account the unquestionable fact that it targeted areas of the city where the only shoes were those its citizens were wearing. It is obvious that those shoes . . .'

Round and round it goes. Report, opium of the people. The world's concern has already shifted. That spare item of news rots in some cranny.

(30 September 1938)

* * *

The Bar

The barman's gaze is ever more philosophical. From beneath a wrinkled brow, it prowls through the air, follows the flight of a fly, focuses vaguely. Finally it glances past me, moves on, returns, spots me, and asks. Coffee. (Or malt, naturally.) Saccharine? No. A stretch! The girl bringing the coffeepot looks like a refugee from Malaga. A stretch! A southern chatterbox. Big curls down her cheeks. Large, sad-ballad eyes. A stretch? Here. She pours out the hot black juice. The Malaguenya lifts her arm and is extremely decorative. The olives, even more so. Three large wooden trays with raised edges along the long white counter. Black olives, on small plates. Tasty bitterness around pleasant pits. The coffee—not malt, maybe coffee—sends a pleasant warmth to the soles of my feet. Tongue and teeth scour the pits, voluptuously.

Olives. Life is sweet. It only needs a slice of crust to ensure complete happiness. A beautiful expanse, dotted black with olives. Hundreds of hands came to harvest. And not all bitterness is tasty. Olive trees. Contorted olive trees. Majorca. Sun, fresh, pure air, golden isle. Italians. A big *sheaf* haunting our flesh. Will they come today? The regulars talk, lean in a line on the counter, gulp their coffee, spit out pits. Will they come today? It's very likely. A couple of yards away in the street, a huge crater left by the last bombing raid. A handful of men are calmly, patiently filling it in. Have you ever seen a perfect darner? She seeks out the thread time and again, lifts it, squints at the eye of the needle level with her nose. Those men, like her, or almost, are darning the road—with rocks, sand, spade, crowbar, and pick. Will they come today? It's very likely. We look at window panes, mirrors, glasses, cups, hot chocolate mugs. A big blast would shatter the lot! 'Each shard', says one citizen, striking a dramatic pose, 'would be a dagger.' And so what? A stretch! The coffee's hot, the bitter olive sweet on the palate. Enjoy while we can.

We enjoy, we squeeze dry the passing moment. Dark pits emerge bare and burnished. Life is beautiful, and the olive-pit atmosphere, seductive. The bar's decor introduces a vital glow. Beautiful trees, large painted harvests seem to come alive. Buxom farmgirls storing apples, oranges, peaches, pears in caves . . . A stretch! There's a large steaming mug of hot chocolate. A beautiful, monstrous wafer sticking out. The motto: hot chocolate with milk. A determined woman strides in. She evidently knows where she's going and what she wants. Hot chocolate, please. Hey, hey! You don't have any? What does it say there? That's right, dear. As we don't have any, we paint some. Ah! Coffee, saccharine? Hey, a stretch!

A punctilious citizen politely declares that coffee and olives don't go together. He wants vermouth. Vermouth? Ah! Don't you have anything similar? Fortified wine? What's that? Forte, fortress, forthwith. With cinchona. What's cinchona? It's a barking cinch that'll give you a winch. Thousands of citizens clench their fists by their ears and sprinkle the revitalizing juice on their heads. But take care. Don't let it drip into your nose or feathers will sprout. My god, what a plonking imagination! Stop that, you're in a bar, try the fortified stuff. Ersatz, the great word of our times! It's not bad at all. It goes with black olives. The two bitter notes play sweetly on the tongue, slip smoothly down the gullet. Will they come? And so what if they do? The girl from Malaga says she's so scared when she hears the sirens. A soldier laughs. And her sad-ballad eyes suddenly sparkle and smile. The barman grins enigmatically and his philosophical gaze prowls through the air, follows the flight of a fly, focuses, beneath his wrinkled brow. At last he spots me. More coffee? Yes, please. A stretch!

(31 December 1938)

A Detective Story

Juan Marsé

Out of small misinterpretations of reality, we construct beliefs and hopes, and live on the crusts of what we call loaves, like poor children playing at being happy.

Fernando Pessoa, *The Book of Disquiet*

On luminous days in the highest reaches of the city, from this street rearing up on the hillside as if wanting to see itself mirrored in the Mediterranean, the eye is lured far across the sea and the heart is easily fooled: the neighbourhood dozes in the sun, witness to a dream that never sparks into life. Yet, sometimes, beyond the port and breakwater, beyond the white foam from the sloops flecking the shoreline, on the poops of cargo ships seemingly anchored to the horizon and the rusty forecastles of huge oil tankers sailing southwards, we have seen silver hoops glitter in the ears of sailors leaning on gunwales, mermaids tattooed on bronze chests, and hearts shot through by arrows beneath a woman's name; that is, if you stare really hard, if you really want to see what you're looking at and don't let yourself be dazzled by the sun.

But on grey days your gaze becomes ensnared in the swirling mist and smoke choking the labyrinthine streets of Horta and La Salud, and you can see no further. The grey city squats in the distance, like a silted pond, like stagnant water.

It was one of those foul, drizzly days when the wind gusted icily that we met in the car to be given our little errands. Through the windscreen we watched a buffeted seagull drift aimlessly by. At times the wind pounded even harder and the rain seemed to hang in the air, silent and oblique. The seagull plummeted towards us, an ashen wing grazing the Lincoln's shattered windscreen, one leaden eye glancing sideways before it swooped up.

'A devil of a day,' said Marés from behind the steering wheel, before he offered us a smoke. 'Keep your eyes peeled.'

He spoke with that ventriloquist's voice of his, never moving his lips. And dreamily, through the bluest, most transparent smoke ever to issue from rancid cigarettes manufactured in the most rancid of times, we saw a woman cross the wasteland towards us; she wore a grey beret and a light-coloured raincoat and was very pale, very pretty, and in tears. It was a Saturday afternoon and an April that seemed more like November.

Juanito Marés scrutinized David and Jaime in the back seat, and turned to me. When he elbowed me in the ribs, I realized I was the chosen one:

> 'Great legs,' he said, looking at the woman.
> 'Yes, boss.'
> 'Like them?'
> 'Sure do, boss.'
> 'Don't let them out of your sight.'

He narrowed his eyes like a wily old Barry Fitzgerald ordering his sidekick to follow the girl in *The Naked City*, and drawled: 'On your way, son, she's all yours.'

She walked past us trailing a bitter scent of onions and tears, maybe even vinegar. Beneath her raincoat hem, cinched tightly at the waist, the fullness of her knees suggested thighs that simply must have rubbed together as she walked. Yet she was slim, with small breasts and slender hips. We hadn't a clue who she was, we'd never seen her before, but the boss had gleaned a few things: that she was new to the area, that she was living in the Pension Ynes with a small child, and that her husband had left her. She called herself Señora Yordi, but rumour had it that it wasn't her real name.

'It's all we got,' concluded Marés, elbowing me again. 'Now get going.'

I chucked my cigarette away, tilted my hat down, and got out of the car, unable to take my eyes off those long legs, so mournful in stockings and the rain, as they crossed a sea of black mud.

A thrilling adventure was about to start, and something told me it wouldn't end well. I stood still for a few seconds next to the hood of the Lincoln under the drizzle. The Campo de la Calva extended before me, a dreary, water-logged esplanade at the end of the street, overlooking the hill dotted with yellow broom. A place so high, so close to the clouds, Marés liked to say, the rain hanging in the air. This hillside platform had been planned as a square but was no more than a mudflat; one side was a string of low houses with Fermín's bar and the paper shop, and the other, nothing at all sloping away to pine and chestnut trees with leafy Vallcarca in the distance. People called it the Campo de la Calva because Franco's Moorish shock troops once played football there with a prostitute's shaven, severed head, and they say they booted and kicked it about so much the head turned smooth and shiny like a billiard ball, no nose, no eyes, no ears, and its jaw loosened and when the game was over, they buried it mouth agape. Much later, we excavated El Campo, but all we found was a dog's skull.

And that was what I was thinking as I watched Señora Yordi walk off.

'What the hell are you waiting for?!' roared the boss, sticking his head out of the window of the Lincoln. 'Off you go, follow her!'

'I reckon this dame spells trouble, boss.'

'Don't be such a smart-ass, Roca. I want a full rundown, so get moving.'

'It's hard to tail such a pretty woman without arousing suspicion.'

'Well, let's see what you can do! Get a move on!'

'All right, I'm off.'

But I stayed rooted to the spot, as if the open jaws of the bald whore under the ground had snapped shut around my ankles. A god-awful, blustery wind whipped bits of paper and laurel leaves down the Bajada de la Gloria. Towards Los Penitentes, on the other side of the Tres Cruces hill, storm clouds broke away from the grey sky like pumice crags.

Marés cursed and I finally set off after Señora Yordi. The chips were down.

As she passed Susana's paper shop and was about to turn the corner, the wind suddenly changed direction and rammed into her, and she leant back as if enjoying lolling on the wind and being swept along for a while: her raincoat clung to her buttocks, her short black bob parted at the nape of her neck as she hung onto her beret. The cooing pigeons, the sweet smell of armpits unnerved me.

The moment she vanished around the corner, I pulled up my jacket collar and went in hot pursuit.

2

I returned two hours later to find Marés still sitting behind the steering wheel. He kicked open the door and I sat down next to him. I saw David and Jaime in the rearview mirror, slumped across the backseat, their hair wet, their eyes feverish. They'd set out on their missions after me, but had finished sooner. It was raining harder.

'I stopped home on the way back,' I said by way of apology. 'OK then. I followed her for three quarters of an hour. She went down the Bajada, along Nuestra Señora del Col and then walked along the Avenida Hospital Militar, on towards Lesseps. She stopped crying.'

Pensive, I lit a cigarette, closing my eyes amid the spirals of smoke, trying to get a better view of the movement of her hips again. 'She's walking with her chin stuck out and her eyes lowered, unhurried, not noticing the rain. We wouldn't feel it on our faces, if the wind hadn't been so fierce, I remember thinking, it's such fine drizzle. She's not crying, but you'd say she's haunted by the bitterest thoughts. No umbrella, a raincoat that's short on her, a couple of inches above the knee, a skirt that's even shorter, hardly a peep of it, a bag on her shoulder, ashen stockings, and high-heels with two black straps twisting and crossing at the ankle.

'She's thirty or so, her high cheeks polished like ivory. Whenever she looks round, behind the soft veil of rain I glimpse dark, almond eyes and sweet oriental eyelids. For a while I'm so close, I can smell the rain on her hair and hear the silk stockings rub between her thighs.'

'When I want personal detail, I'll let you know,' said Marés curtly. 'Go on.'

'We walk past Las Cañas bar, the Mahón cinema, the butcher's in the square, the dry-cleaners, and Falange Party Offices. As she walks, ill-shaven men stagger and stare, rummage in their trouser pockets, and mutter hoarse obscenities. Perhaps trying to drive away her sadness, she stops in front of a shop window and looks at her reflection, smooths her wind-swept hair, adjusts her beret, takes a red lipstick from her handbag and drags it across her lips, and finally rubs her waxen eyelids that are so still and mysterious, with the tip of her ring finger. She looks surprisingly like Fah lo Suee, the daughter of Fu Manchu: the very same eyes as that salacious, steamy China girl.

'I wanted to get a better look and stopped really close. I stooped down and pretended to tie my shoelaces,' I added in my nasal, detective voice, catching the boss's scornful snort, out of the corner of my eye. 'But then she turns around unexpectedly, and gives me a silent, icy stare. My heart skips a beat. Hell, those eyes! I look away, at a tramp hobbling along behind a baby's pram piled high with bottles and dirty rags. Poor devil, he stumbles against the kerb and almost falls over.'

I broke off my report to take a couple of drags on my cigarette, and behind me David let out a thick, hacking cough smelling of cheap jam made from carobs or God knows what. I pondered how to continue my tale as I watched the rain bounce off the hood of the 1941 Lincoln Continental with aerodynamic lines and a chrome radiator that had come from somewhere or other to die here like a load of scrap metal. A glimmer of its past splendour lingered amid the rust and broken glass, but without wheels or engine, the whole thing looked like the huge charred torso of a legless cockroach, and nobody in the area could remember how or when it had come to rest there, who had abandoned it on this small hill to the north-west of the city, or why. The Lincoln was stranded in that sea of black mud and fenced in by a heap of lifeless objects: bits of iron cooker, a gutted armchair, stacks of tyres, rusty bedsprings, and torn, filthy mattresses.

'A bit further down, in front of the Roxy, the one-armed guy is selling tobacco and matches under an umbrella, and, hell, the bastard accosts her with a stream of muck. She crosses to the other pavement, heading down Calle

Salmerón. And she didn't look back once. Then I saw something that made my hair stand on end: a tram almost knocks her over.'

I was only telling them what had happened, but the best was what I would have liked to happen, the things I imagined while I tracked her so closely, drinking in the smell of moss from her hair. You know, the tram knocks her over, her head bangs against the cobblestones and she loses consciousness. She's on the ground, face up, in a white satin dressing-gown and pink-tasselled slippers, the traffic stops, a crowd gathers around her, someone asks for a doctor, and a voice says she needs mouth-to-mouth resuscitation, quick, and is there anybody who knows how? In her unconscious state, the victim points to me, begging me to be the one to give her a mouth-to-mouth.

'Hey, you got the short straw,' said David, 'I wouldn't have done it for all the tea in China.'

And I volunteer and give the lady a mouth-to-mouth with the blessing of all present. Her lips are as cold as silk-worms, and it is my strangest, most unforgettable kiss ever. Her mouth opens and releases a wave of heat, a taste of red lips and rippling folds of fleshy affection that blossom like a vulva or a flower. As the kiss was ending, her smouldering, scheming China-girl eyes flicker open and stare straight into mine. The rain is reflected, bulges, in her luminous eyes, ruffled by a breeze, as in a miniature.

3

The fleeting evening light, glides, here and now, like a golden bird over the sea of mud.

'Nothing happened until just before the Rambla del Prat,' I went on. She met someone she wasn't expecting in front of the Estadio bar. Charles Lafiton, the baker, who was standing on the edge of the pavement waiting to cross, turns and smiles at Sra Yordi, dripping chops and triple chins like the disgusting slimy toad he is. Hey, fancy seeing you here? A long way from our neck of the woods? And in this lousy weather. And she pretends she's not narked, and answers nervously, though pleasantly enough. Well, I just came to buy an umbrella . . . A lie, as we'll see soon enough.

'I stop and crouch down behind a postbox, but fat Lafiton sees me, and she does too, again. That's inevitable, if I want to stay close and find out what they're talking about. Through the drizzle now swept by the wind, grey and wiry like the hairs of a rat, my eyes are glued to the eyes of Sra Yordi, who says: "Look at that kid. He's been following me from the top of Calle Verdi."

'Charles Lafiton screws up his small, piggy eyes and eyes me for a while, his hands clasped behind his back and his short legs apart, as if he was standing on the deck of the *Bounty* with Captain Bligh's bestial face and that disgusting wart on his cheek.

'"Mmm," he grunts. "I'd swear that it's Berta's pesky son. Last Sunday him and his gang of ragamuffin mates were following me when I was taking a stroll near Sants station."

'Hear that? The bastard calls it strolling when he's black-marketing sacks of flour. But she's so discreet and patient, so mysterious and oriental in the drizzle, she ignores his nonsense. And says: "Oh, really? So they followed you too? Why was that?"

'"For no reason at all. It's just a game."

'"What kind of game?"

'"Detectives, spies," the baker grunts. "They pick on somebody walking down the street and follow them for hours."

'"Well, I say," she says, suspicious not of me, but of that leery fat guy smiling sarcastically all over his sea-bream mouth and staring at her trying to guess what she's thinking. "Now isn't that a hoot?"'

'As you know,' I added, 'I can understand what people are saying from that distance because when I was a kid I learned to lip-read.'

'Yes, we know all about that,' David snapped.

I looked at Marés the boss. He was listening thoughtfully and tight-lipped, his arms resting on the steering wheel and looking ahead, beyond the blind windscreen. He had lit another of his famous anisette Virginia Player cigarettes that he carried in a pale blue metal tin, and David coughed out another lump of stone grey slime. Jaime slapped him on his doubled-up back and protested: '*Sacré bleu*! How can you smoke that rubbish?'

'It smells of anisette.'

'It smells of burnt rope sandals. It stinks.'

'It's the car that stinks,' I told him.

'It's one hundred percent shit,' insisted Jaime. 'Why don't you buy Ideales once in a while?'

'Shut up,' ordered the boss without raising his voice. 'Finish your damned report, Roca. And try to get to the point.'

'Yes, boss.'

'Looking so clever-clever, the fat baker goes on spinning words to Sra Yordi: "Well, that's what those rascals say. That they're playing at spies and secret agents. Or conmen and rip-off merchants, God knows."

'"You don't mean that!"

'"Take a look at the hat he's wearing. It belonged to his father, who's inside for conning and because he was a red and a separatist."

'She looks at him for a second with real hatred in her eyes. It's difficult to glimpse that in oriental eyes that always look at everything with a perverse, almost syphilitic sweetness, a kind of pus in their pupils, you bet because they've seen so much wretchedness in this life, but *I* knew what he meant. And I also got the frosty chill in her voice when she replied: "How can you say such a thing, Sr Oms."

'"They're evil people, the whole neighbourhood knows that."

'Sra Yordi was going to respond, but thought better of it. Finally, in a more easy-going tone, she said: "After all, it's only kids playing a game."

'"Even so it shows a lack of upbringing to follow you, especially a lady like yourself. If this boy is annoying you, get a policeman . . ."

'"No, I will not."

'Annoyed, she turns to leave. It's so nice to watch the blurred pink of her lips while she says goodbye time and again to that pain Lafiton, but not succeeding. Because that fatty with the eyes of a poisonous frog never stops spouting: "They're layabouts and good-for-nothings, they spend the whole bloody day in billiard halls and in the street or the cinema, or curled up like little chicks inside that clapped-out, flea-ridden automobile beached in the mud and rubbish, a nest of beggars, smoking and planning chases and pursuits in the corrupt, mysterious city, sniffing crimes in the fog and tailing suspects in the rain, while a ship's horn blasts in the distance seeking permission to enter the port."'

On stormy days like today, ships' horns made us think of French whores leaning on lampposts at night, with their black satin skirts slit down the side.

'"Let them be, they're only kids playing at being in a movie," she replied. "And goodbye, I'll be late."

'"Not true, señora, they're real hoodlums," that bastard of a black-marketeering baker was working himself up, "they won't grow up little saints on the shit that's eating them!"

'"Hey, you just calm down."

'"It starts with toy pistols and movie hold-ups. Bullets of spit and fake murders. But one day the bullets and murders will be for real, señora, like that kid's hat. You wait till they grow up. They'll be worse than the plague."'

'Blasted Captain Bligh,' muttered David. 'Fuck you!'

'Yes, why doesn't the sea swallow him up?'

'He's a big mouth,' said Marés. 'A big nark, just ignore him.'

'But he goes around saying that his father is in La Modelo and criticizing his hat into the bargain,' said Jaime, 'and that's real nasty.'

'Ignore him,' the boss insisted. 'OK, Lafiton is a rotten piece of work, but we'll deal with him one of these days. Now carry on, Roca.'

'When he told Sra Yordi about my father being in jail, I lowered my head, took off my hat and hid it between my chest and my shirt: not because I was ashamed, but because I was so furious. It's a very flexible hat, a good make, a genuine Stetson, just the thing for pursuing dangerous blondes on rainy days. I hid it for a moment, for my father, out of respect for his memory as a republican gunman and separatist red with its flexible brim over your eyes . . .'

'Well done,' said David. 'You only have one father, even if he's in the slammer.'

'Or in the bar and drunk the whole fucking day, like one I know,' lamented Jaime.

'Are you done, you chatterboxes?' said Marés, impatiently wiping what was left of the windscreen glass with an angry fist. 'So go on, Roca. What else could you read from their lips? What else, for Christ's sake?'

'Well, then she finally starts walking backwards, starts to leave, leaving the gossipy baker mouthing furiously. "What do you still not have any news of your husband?" Lafiton whispers leering at her hips: "Hell, these nosey kids following us when we clear off a while, and spying on our secret doings through the keyhole . . . they're really evil, aren't they, señora? And sometimes it's a really compromising situation for a married woman, don't you think?"'

'Did he really say all that?' the boss asked.

'More or less. Sometimes the rain didn't let me read their lips. What matters is the sense of what he said. But she ignores him and goes down the righthand side of Salmerón.

'Trampled stems of carnations and gladioli stalks lay on the damp asphalt at the crossroads with Travesera, and a rabid blindman banging his stick on the kerb, waiting for someone to help him over to the other side, spitting at the clouds. And a smell of warm bread on the corner of Luis Antúñez, and a bit further down my other favourite smell, of dried cod and seasoned olives in little barrels on the pavement. I let my claw drop as I walk by and fish out a fistful of olives, I walk on down and in front of me a beggar is dragging a wicker basket along with a piece of rope and inside a kid wrapped in rags is squatting on empty champagne bottles. The kid's bleary eyes look at me while we walk along and smiles and sticks his tongue out and I throw him olives which he catches one after another opening his mouth like a jam jar.

'We walk by the Cine Mundial and the lady stops in front of the Bar Monumental. Before she goes in, she looks suspiciously right and left. I wait for a few minutes and go in after her.

'Sra Yordi is sitting with a plump, swarthy guy at a corner table towards the back of that swell bar, behind the billiard tables. Two serious young men with smart haircuts are playing on one of the tables; they're wearing plus fours, and playing very careful shots, with lots of guile. I walk over pretending to be surprised by their just-so style and keep an eye on the couple from there, whispering quietly in the shadows. The man is older, around forty, dark glasses, a raven's beak, neatly trimmed moustache and a toothpick between his teeth. Head down, keeping her hands in her raincoat pockets, she looks at her knees she's pulled tight together and doesn't say a word. The bloke talks in her ear, with his arm on the back of her chair, not touching her, but as if he were dying to do exactly that. The light is so poor I can't make out his lips, and barely the movement of the toothpick the guy's tongue shifts from one side to the other.

'Then I look hard and catch what he's saying: "I'll do what I can, señora, I promise . . ." The only sound to be heard is of billiard balls hitting each other. She remains silent, and he says: "Trust me, señora, don't get carried away by despair, it will sort itself out, I have friends with influence . . ." or something of the sort.

'I took good care she didn't see me,' I said. 'It was easy, she kept her eyes on the ground, she seemed embarrassed.

'Ten minutes later they both left the bar and stopped a taxi. They left in a hurry and the last I saw of her was her open hand pressing against the car window as if someone was forcing her to kiss him, or was strangling her.'

4

Juanito Marés drummed his fingers on the steering wheel and looked out. The wind had stopped but the clouds were rushing in packs across the gloomy sky, and the evening gleamed a clay-red, as if it were about to rain mud.

'Which way did the taxi go?'

'Up,' I said, 'Plaza Lesseps.'

'OK.' Maré looked for David's face in the rearview mirror. 'Your turn now, David. Tell us it as it was.'

David cleared his throat before deciding to speak. He stared at me. He started his report with a statement that surprised me: 'The man I followed was following you when you were following that lady. Nervy and intrigued, he added: 'He walked past here just after you'd gone after her, and the boss gave me my orders: follow that man. The guy trailed you as far as the Bar Monumental. He stopped when you stopped, he waited for you when there was the encounter with Charles Lafiton, he changed pavement when you did. The whole lot.'

'Crikey!'

'And he always kept the same distance, about twenty metres.'

'Fantastic! But you're inventing all this, David.'

'Jaime saw it too. He'll say if I'm lying.'

The boss didn't open his mouth. We looked at him, awaiting his verdict. He only said: 'Describe him.'

'Smallish, a bit of a big head, medium to small build, around thirty-five, black, flattened hair, with a centre parting and a paper-white face, made up, old-fashioned and charming as if he used rouge and brilliantine, as if one day he'd been the bee's knees, high society and rich, or very loved and happy, far from here, in another district and another era. From close-up you see the pallor of his face comes from rice-powder makeup, and his thin, black lips look like painted wooden lips. He's carrying a lady's umbrella with an ivory handle inset with silver and precious stones, though one spoke is broken, and is wearing a black overcoat over striped pyjamas and felt house slippers, as if he'd just left a theatre stage to buy a newspaper on the street corner.'

'When you went into the Monumental,' David went on, 'he stood there on the pavement, closed his umbrella and I thought he'd go in too. But he didn't. He stayed there like a statue, staring at the door.

'By his side, at the top of an alley, a young layabout with an aviator's or biker's glasses on his forehead and a shabby military blanket over his shoulders slips slowly by, his back against a lamp post and then collapses onto the ground, hands in pockets, smiling at passers-by. They put him up against the wall and hit him, but he doesn't react: he keeps his eyes open and his hands in his trouser pockets, as if he was fine, on top of the world, but doesn't react.

'The man with the make-up and pyjamas under an overcoat ignored everything around him, had eyes only for the bar-door,' said David. 'He suddenly went up to the door and his mug hit the glass.

'He kept his nose stuck up against the glass for a while, and when he moved away, he looked like a changed person. As if he'd aged twenty years at a stroke. As if he'd seen a ghost. He dejectedly crossed the street and miraculously reached the other pavement, as a tram almost ran into him. And he twisted around and stood there on the kerb staring at the bar-door with the closed umbrella under his armpit, getting soaked like an idiot, his pale make-up streaming down his death-head's cheeks. His feet splashed in his slippers under the muddy bottoms of his pyjama trousers. Then he retreated into a shop doorway, but didn't do so because of the rain, so as not to get wet, but because he didn't want people to see him crying like a kid abandoned at the edge of a stream. People walked by and took no notice of him.

'Then his trembling hand takes a handkerchief from his pocket and his wallet falls to the ground. He doesn't notice, or isn't worried. He's like a man gone crazy, with a screw loose.'

For some time it had been obvious that David wasn't enjoying telling that pathetic tale. He cut his conclusion short: the sad man with rouged cheeks tired of whimpering and left. He wandered aimlessly along Gracia's dirty side streets like an old geezer who's lost his mind and stepped into the lobby of the Cine Delicias and lit a cigarette, which he threw down almost immediately and went up to the projection room and spoke for moment with the projectionist, he left the door open, and you could hear their voices and the voices from the film, then he came back down, even more despondently, resumed his walk and ended up sitting and gawping in the entrance to a big house on Calle Legalidad.

'That's when I left him and came back here,' said David, struggling to control a fresh outbreak of coughing he'd been storing in his lungs. 'And that was that. The end.'

'What about his wallet?'

'Here it is.'

It was fake crocodile skin, small, and so flat it seemed it must be empty. But inside there were five *duro* notes and a battered yellow photograph taken by an itinerant photographer where you could see pigeons and a very blurred soldier and girl holding hands. The photo was falling to bits and smelt dusty. The impact of an ancient sun frozen on the young couple's faces blurred their features and all that endured was the glimmer of a smile, a spectral flutter of lashes, a remnant of happiness.

5

David coughed again and looked for an approving gesture from his boss. He was still a novice, but perhaps this piece of work would finally earn him his credentials.

Marés was deep in thought. He clicked his tongue and said: 'That's OK. Here you are.'

He took a card from his pocket and gave it to him. Written in invisible ink, it said:

> David Bartra. Donald Lam/Berta Cool Detective Agency. Enquiries, trailing, secret missions, sabotage. C/Verdi, Campo de la Calva, no number.

'But just so you know, you've not earned it,' Marés added. 'Your report was poor from the first word, because it's based on a mistaken deduction.'

'Mistaken?'

'Yes.'

Marés lit up another of his perfumed cigarettes and gave David a sly glance through the rearview window. He said: 'Just think with your brain, kid.'

'I do, boss.'

'Let's see then. Based on the data we have, not just yours, but Roca's as well on Sra Yordi, how would you proceed?'

David lifted his hand up, looked at the red ends of his fingers and stammered: 'Mmm, I don't know.'

The boss looked at him and wrinkled his nose. The back seats gave off a sour stink. At night tramps used to sleep in the Lincoln hugging their sticky bottles of wine.

'What do you reckon, Jaime?'

'It's a complex business, boss.'

Marés waited a bit, in case Jaime wanted to put forward his theory, and then he looked at me.

'What about you? Have you got any idea?'

'I've got one, but I'm not altogether sure.'

'Out with it, lad.'

'I don't know,' I said, shrugging my shoulders. 'I don't want to bore the pants off you, boss.'

'Bore the pants off me. And that's an order.'

I cleared my throat, and in a cold, neutral voice, I ventured an explanation.

'This lady has a bit on the side because she needs to buy food for her kid, and because she's alone, she hasn't got a husband. She meets her lover in that bar. The taxi went to the rooming house, La Casita Blanca. And that man with the make-up, with his striped pyjamas and felt slippers was following her because he's a pansy.'

Marés purred like a cat rehearsing his fake voice and took a few seconds to answer: 'You've almost got it right,' the smoke from his cigarette forced him to half-close his eyes, together with his habitual cunning and bad blood. Now he's again speaking without moving his lips, and his cold, artificial voice seemed to come from afar, from other zones of feeling, like the voice of a ventriloquist. 'Yes, everything points to the idea that the guy in the pyjamas was following you, Roca. But, in fact, he was following her. You placed yourself in between them, and he didn't even see you. He was following her, just as you were, but at a distance, and always behind you.' He looked at David in the rearview mirror. 'Anyone would have realized that except for a novice like you, David. Just think for a minute: why would this gent walk that way as if he was sleepwalking, stalking Mingo Roca, a local chav you can bet he'd never seen before? Why would he?'

David looked down and muttered apologetically: 'Well once, a stranger followed me from Atracciones Apolo to Monte Caramelo.'

'That must have been a bugger.'

'And how do you know this guy isn't?'

'Because I know them all.' He stayed silent for a few seconds and added: 'Can you think of any other explanation?'

He lolled back rippling like a caterpillar and put his feet on the steering wheel, took off a shoe and sock, and scratched between his toes. Then raising his stinking hoof till it touched his nose, he pincered the cigarette hanging from the scabby corner of his mouth between his big toe and the next and carried on smoking quietly with his foot, his hands crossed behind the back of his neck. He was half contortionist, half ventriloquist, skills he had been taught by old workmates of his mother, broke, unemployed music-hall artists.

'OK. Let's recapitulate.'

He always used the same words and behaved in the same way, delaying the solution to the riddle as long as he could. When he'd listened to our reports, Marés changed into the Spider-That-Smokes and meditated awhile surrounded in a cloud of smoke from the fag he deftly handled with his foot. He analysed all the data, dissected them, asked for apparently banal detail, and, finally, after rejecting our suggestions, imposed his own criteria via deductions that were generally convincing, based on cause and effect, and granting the behaviour of suspects, however enigmatic, motives we had never predicted, and that were almost always bitterly disheartening. From early childhood he had given indications of that strange, terrible facility: you could say he intuited the secret misfortunes and bitterness almost everybody bore with resignation in their heart of hearts; you could say he discerned the memory of a recent humiliation just by watching people's faces, or from the way they walked or stopped in the street and stooped over something, just a small detail. One day when we saw Sr Elías weeping in the bar, sitting alone in a corner and listening to a military march on the radio, Marés said the man was crying because the radio reminded him that a daughter of his was working as a whore in Saragossa, behind an infantry barracks where a brigade was rearing a thousand pigs on leftover grub. And it was true, it was confirmed by Jaime's elder brother when he came back from military service and told us about Puri! And the thousand hogs fed on leftovers from the barracks kitchen was true as well!

At the end of the day, Juanito Marés was quite a bit older than us, had been brought up here and was Catalan, as well as being something of a contortionist and a ventriloquist: he was more serious, spoke more languages, had studied more. That was why he was the boss.

6

When Marés started talking, I looked through the Lincoln side window at a huge fist-shaped, leaden cloud surging angrily against the sky from the blurred horizon of the sea, far from the port, at the frontiers with the Orient. I thought of the murky fate in the rain of the lady with the Chinese eyes, and of the horrible fate met by the whore whose bald, severed head lay buried beneath us: life and death strangely united in the same solitude and same adolescent fever, in the single flesh of a woman who had figured in dreams, had been subjugated and finally destroyed. And I felt dizzy thinking deliriously of all that, and was suddenly deafened or shell-shocked. I took fright and interrupted Marés: 'So, boss, what are we going to do with the wallet, the photo, and the money?'

'Let David keep them for the moment.' Juanito Marés looked at me for a second and then continued: 'I was saying that the man with the broken umbrella and rice powder on his face must be a theatre actor. And, what's more, that he is her husband, the real Sr Yordi, who they say left his wife some time ago. And don't ask me anything else right now, it's a hunch . . . First of all, let's be clear that Yordi isn't a surname: Yordi is the way you immigrants pronounce Jordi, and it is the husband's real first name in Catalan, and not his surname, that I would swear is Jardí. Have you got that, you illiterate sods, you unschooled natives, you fucking Murcians?'

Curled up at the back of the Lincoln, David and Jaime blinked anxiously and Marés went on: '. . .because this wretch who starts whimpering in the street, in front of the bar where she has a date with her fancy man, is obviously her husband. And, as he is an actor, and on Saturdays and Sundays performs in an amateur theatre, one of the many in the neighbourhood, in L'Artesà, or Els Teixidors or the Orfeó Gracienc, where you bet he plays bit parts as a refined, mature gallant in the manner of Charles Boyer, with silvery temples, bootees, and gloves, and often leaves home already made up and dressed for the show, as most actors do; perhaps he does that because he prefers to be anonymous at street level, to go disguised as someone else, to *be* someone else,' added Marés thoughtfully, 'many down on their luck actors dream of being someone else . . . It all fits: local gossip says he left his wife, but in fact he left her in order to hide in another house, because someone informed on him and the cops are on his trail. And madly in love with his wife, suspecting she is going to meet another man, this afternoon jealousy diverted him from his normal route to the theatre and guided him to the pension Ynes, where he waited for her to leave and then followed her.'

'It all fits,' he repeated, scratching his ear with his big toe. 'What do you reckon, do you agree?'

We nodded.

'Only the poor wretch gets it all wrong,' Marés went on. 'She's not deceiving him out of pleasure, because *he* is a poor devil and a failure. The guy waiting for her by the Monumental billiard tables isn't really a lover or a fancy man she dotes on. Who is he then? Why do they meet secretly?'

'Hell, what do you think?' I smiled sarcastically. 'The bloke is mad about her legs, he can't keep his hands off her. At this very minute, boss, he is fucking her like crazy.'

'Perhaps. But he isn't her lover or heart-throb. When have you ever seen a women in love turn up looking so miserable and listless, and sobbing, to a date with her lover? I tell you it's something else. Didn't you see her darned stockings, her short raincoat with its belt pulled so tight under her breasts, and those *femme fatale* shoes that don't suit such a refined lady, that make her totter so badly? Don't you conclude that she wants to seduce someone, to do whatever it takes, seduce quickly and perversely, and then dress in quite another style? You've got to see her like I'm seeing her, lads, do me a bloody favour and imagine her differently, if you really want to shine in this gumshoe business. Come on, push yourselves, make more of an effort to tie up the loose ends and draw some bold conclusions, learn to be more observant and devious, or you'll never make it . . .

'Now let's consider the guy the lady's seeing,' he added, lowering his voice, 'this fancy man with the toothpick and hooked nose sitting in the gloomiest spot in the bar, behind the billiard tables, like a vulture about to pounce on carrion. He sits there, in a black leather jacket with velvet lapels on his shoulders and gloved hand swollen by rings the size of bunions when he raises his glass of Fundador. Who is he, a black marketeer, a flamboyant administrator from the Supplies Commission, a cop, or a pimp? How did you describe him, Roca, have you forgotten already? I haven't: a flash guy who likes to brag, blue shirt, little black tash, lacquer and brilliantine on his zeppelin head, and dark glasses. Didn't you see the black spidery badge on his lapel. Because he is a Falangist, you bet he is, a bright spark with friends in high places, a Flecha who's got the cow by the teat and ain't letting go. And what's she after from that imperial comrade, what can a woman married to a third-rate actor who has only ever acted in local fleapits possibly want from a man like that? Well, obviously, a favour, an endorsement, for her husband. Because he's a member of the Falange who's well connected and ready to hand out favours, especially to a lonely, desperate woman, and we know he had influence, and can get a certificate of good behaviour, a recommendation, whatever she asks him for.

'"Trust in my discretion, señora, I'll do what I can," you say he told her with his claw on her knee. I mean, it all fits so nicely.'

But we weren't so sure.

'What?' I said suddenly, thinking straight. All that seemed like a leg-pull, a big con. 'Come on, boss. That's going too far.'

I looked through the drizzle and, for some reason or other, started to think of the chilly, promiscuous city spreading out below us under a cloak of mist, the long Saturday queues outside the heated cinemas, or the packed trams going down the Ramblas, the men huddling in the lobbies of whorehouses, the cheerful girls in their brightly coloured macs walking arm-in-arm into dance halls. And we were up here, daydreaming.

Sickened by the story and the smell of ne'er-do-wells stinking out the car, we stayed silent, for a second time in a few minutes, completely disagreeing with the boss. We hadn't discussed it, but the three of us thought the same: this time his famous deductions had gone too far.

'It's all very odd and far too contrived,' muttered Jaime. 'And it can't be so contrived . . .'

'It isn't. It's very simple.'

'Mmm,' reacted David. 'And why on earth does that crybaby, idiot clown have to be her husband?'

'Yes,' I agreed. 'Why does he? I reckon he's just a drunk who's fled his home in his pyjamas, who doesn't have a cent and that's why he's crying, because he can't go into the bar and order a glass of wine.'

Marés smiled at us sarcastically: 'But didn't he have five *duros* in his wallet?'

'One thing is for sure,' reflected David. 'He's not living with her and the boy in the pension. Perhaps he just came to pay them a visit, but, why in his pyjamas? Where was he coming from? Roca says that after wandering around there he saw him go into a big house on Calle Legalidad. That's quite a long way to go.'

'He lives there because he's hiding from the cops,' deduced Marés dramatically. 'That's blindingly obvious.'

'Don't go shooting in the dark, Coyote,' I told him.

He didn't respond. He closed his fist and nibbled his knuckles.

'Where's your proof, boss?' murmured David, slapping him on the back. 'We don't have any.'

Marés was deep in thought. He held his hand over his mouth like a small trumpet, and hummed a strange, disturbing melody. That melody always haunted him like sadness at twilight, like a deep pain, sudden exhaustion, or an illness. His mother was a medium and fortune teller and had performed in bohemian dives and cabarets when she was young, and on Saturday nights she welcomed into her house two down-at-heel married couples, retired tenors, and chorus girls and they sang operetta and got drunk on wine, wept lyrically around an old piano into the early hours accompanied by other eccentric remnants from show business who we found fascinating: old romancers, obese music-hall stars, starving Aragonese jota dancers, and unemployed magicians who did conjuring tricks. Fu Ching the magician was toothless, consumptive, and an alcoholic, but he still dazzled us with his elegant tricks, precise gestures, and cold air of authority.

A lightning flash fleetingly lit up a vault of clouds scattering in the sky and then Marés's fake voice clashed with the thunder: 'Only a man who is madly in love can follow a woman through the rain like that, crying, in his pyjamas and slippers, made up like a dummy in a house of wax,' he drawled, 'following her down streets as if driven by a fever, by a sickly fantasy,' and he whispered emphatically: 'In love with a woman even beyond the grave.'

His distant, ventriloquizing voice went on vamping up the story with dark stuff from the storm. He inspected the Lincoln's windscreen, now clean—it had stopped raining—as if he were watching a film on a cinema screen, and finally shut up.

David shifted uneasily in his seat.

'All right, boss, let's imagine for a minute that that is what's behind this case . . .'

'I don't believe it,' Jaime interrupted. 'I mean, we're not little kids anymore.'

'But even if it were true,' David insisted, 'we've got no proof.'

'Shut up!' came the order from Marés. 'Who's in charge of investigations?' We all stayed silent, and he added: 'Well then, things are as I said they are. The case is solved. Get out. It's all over.'

He eased slightly back in his seat and curled up, crossing his feet over the scruff of his neck, and I noticed his drowsy feline eyes stare at me, as if expecting a sign of support from me. He'd gone off on one of his intrepid flights of fancy, and, for a second, I thought his angry shaven head reeked of gunpowder. David and Jaime were silently alighting from the car, almost reproachfully. I got out too, and slamming the battered door shut, I said: 'Let's see what tomorrow brings, boss.'

We left him alone in the Lincoln, hunched up behind the curtain of smoke from his fake scented cigarettes. Under a foot that quietly dangled out of the window, whose rusty, dented door lit up a piece of miraculously burnished steel plate that briefly reflected the silhouette of a distant, ragged city, asleep under a shattered sky.

7

Early next morning, a Sunday, some residents on Calle Legalidad gathered on the corner with Escorial, alerted by the hysterical shouts of two girls who were going to mass and saw something that froze their blood. Marés sent a boy with a message and we raced there, but when we arrived, there were so many people in the street we couldn't locate him straight away.

You got a perfect view if you looked up from the pavement on the other side of the street: by the edge of a terrace belonging to an old two-storey house, beneath a small wooden gallery, a hanged man was slowly gyrating in the air, his head lolling on his shoulder and his tongue hanging out, big and black like a shoe. I only had to look into David's shocked eyes for a second, who had seen the dead man close up in the rain only yesterday, to confirm my horrified suspicion. Jaime identified him immediately as well. Shaking, bunched together, and holding hands, as if scared we'd get lost in the crowd, we made our way through until we were in the front row and could stare from there, half in amazement, half incredulously, at the felt slippers on the rigid feet that were still swaying, at the tattered, muddy pyjama bottoms, his smooth, black, impeccably combed hair with a parting down the centre and silvery temples. An old-fashioned, elegant suicide, with the remains of rouge still on his cheeks and black stains under his eyes, he certainly looked as if he was somebody else in another life, in another story from another era, a true gentleman who had escaped from another performance on another stage. Who knows how long he'd been hanging there, dead, truly dead and yet, suddenly, he let out a belch that everyone gathered there could hear perfectly.

First the powers-that-be arrived, then a black van. The hanged man gyrated on the rope and the slipper fell off his left foot, bounced against the stone rail and dropped into the street. A resident picked it up carefully between the tips of his index finger and thumb, as if afraid he might catch something, carried it to the entrance to the house, and left it leaning against the wrought-iron gate, as if to dry in the sun.

Suddenly, all these simple details of the tragedy seemed incomprehensible, and we needed Juanito Marés. It was only after they had hauled down the corpse and the bystanders started to wander off, that we saw him calmly leaning on one side of the funeral van, smiling sarcastically our way. The van drove off and Marés sat on the pavement, contorting. By the time we reached him, he'd changed into a scorpion.

8

A week later, on the Campo de la Calva, we plucked up our courage, stopped the lady in the short raincoat, and handed over the wallet. The boss compelled us to do that, insisting that the hanged man's wallet now belonged to his widow, and nobody should argue with him, because he would beat them up. That was his final order, and we obeyed it when our pockets were full of piping hot chickpeas that we'd just lifted from a shop on Calle Sostres.

'Señora, this is yours,' David said, offering her the crocodile-skin wallet as he looked down at the ground, in the most strangulated, miserable wheeze of a voice we'd ever heard. 'He dropped it in the street.'

She was wearing the same grey beret, the same black shoes and the same handbag, but wore no lipstick and looked taller. She opened the wallet and saw the five *duros*, then she looked lingeringly at the photo of the soldier and the girl under the musty, ancient sun that blurred them like acid. She didn't deny or admit those things belonged to her; she said nothing, barely looked at us, barely smiled at us. Her delicate nose fleetingly caught a whiff of the hot chickpeas coming out of our pockets, and her slanted eyes gazed at the old photo a moment longer, we saw them flutter slowly and sweetly, then she shut the wallet, put it in her pocket, muttered 'thank you', and went on her way.

Those fantastic days of danger and evil finally became our distant past, and now nobody remembers their stench of gunpowder and carrion or our intrepid vocation as detectives. I have sometimes thought back to the hanged man with his slippers and brilliantine, gyrating slowly and stiffly on that rope, as if he wanted to coil up and disappear into the air, I have thought back to his homely slipper bouncing on the street, and to the lady with the slanted eyes of a hot, perverse China girl still staring at that money as if it had rained down from heaven for her . . . At the end of the day, in that era, five *duros* were five *duros*. But most of all I think back to Juanito Marés crouching in the rusted chassis of that Lincoln Continental, all alone, his feet round the scruff of his neck, surrounded by the purest blue smoke from his aromatic liquorice cigarettes, drunk on crime and dangerous widows, entangled plots and star-crossed loves.

EL TANGO
LA GUARDIA VIEJA
La trama nupcial
LLEGAT
Marian Keyes
DIARI del Greg
Harry Potter

The Three Steps

Miquel Molina

When I got back to Barcelona I read lots of novels set in the city. The last five years I'd spent as a postgraduate in foreign universities had helped me to see the city's shortcomings, but also made me nostalgic in the only way you can for the city where you grew up, its streets, the landscapes of your emotional coming of age.

It was the recent novel by a renowned author that most took me back to my adolescent years—and so vividly. While I read his wonderful book, I was reminded of why and in what circumstances I would spend whole afternoons on the top of the Montaña Pelada, the bare, ochre hill that looks arrogantly down on Parc Güell and the El Carmelo district. I remembered how years ago I climbed up there when I was lonely and realized that girls weren't queueing outside my door to go out with me. Then I'd pick a book and take the path to the top feeling very high-minded. After walking for a quarter of an hour, I'd sit down and start to read. Or at least pretend to. In fact, I was too anxious about the image of myself I was projecting to concentrate on the plot and characters. When some tourists who'd wandered off the beaten track or a girl glanced at me out of the corner of their eyes, I tried to guess what they were thinking. Here's an interesting young man who prefers reading in his favourite retreat to wasting his time bar crawling.

When this happened, I perked up briefly, although such an absurd attitude inevitably led to melancholy, which was why my adolescent afternoons always fizzled out.

So one April morning, years after, I decided to revisit that peak. The previous night I had finished reading the novel that took place on my magic mountain. Set in the post-civil-war years, it focused on the drama of the victors and the vanquished. The main characters were three youngsters from poor backgrounds who met every afternoon on rudimentary steps someone had gouged out of a big white rock near the top where they invented their future, with the city at their feet. If one imagined he was going to be a doctor, he pointed to the Hospital de Sant Pau, looking seawards to the left. Another tried to convince his friends he would be wealthy, never detailing exactly how that would happen, while wagging his finger knowingly in the direction of the north upper side. The third, obviously the author's favourite, simply waved the back of his hand in a semi-circle encompassing the whole city. This was the lad who aspired to be mayor or civil governor, or hold any other post that enabled him to subject the citizens of Barcelona to his whims.

With those pages fresh in my mind I climbed the hill and went round the old hermitage in El Carmelo trying to revive my memories of those three steps. Because they *were* real. I'd often seen them and even sat on them, although I wasn't sure if they'd been carved out by human hand or it was the erosion of the rock that had chiselled their edges. I anticipated finding them hidden by bracken and feared it would be a struggle to find them.

I was surprised to see so many tourists on the path. They prompted contradictory reactions. On the one hand, I was annoyed so many people were tramping up and down my secret mountain. On the other, I was pleased that the best vantage point in the city was finally being honoured. Because that was what it was, no doubt about it. It's true it wasn't as impressive as the Tibidabo but it did offer a 360 degree view of Barcelona. It didn't offer the historic heritage of the nearby anti-aircraft batteries from the war, but you could drive to them, which took all the charm away. What I most liked up there was the sense of being on a peak in the Pyrenees, yet surrounded by a sea of houses and streets.

It was early, but five or six people were already on the top; two were athletes having a breather before making their descent. I too rested for a minute. I looked surreptitiously at the hump where I'd sat so many afternoons pretending to read, and then repeated a ritual I'd long forgotten: I glanced across to the distant cemeteries of Sant Andreu and Poblenou, where my grandparents were buried. Years ago, when I was training for a race, a rather gloomy thought had struck me: however far you run, however many exotic places you visit, your bones will end up in one of those niches. Or someone will scatter your ashes over this very mountain. So don't run away. Don't even try to.

The steps.

I walked a couple of yards down from the top. There they were, just as in the novel and exactly where I thought I'd left them the last time, not overgrown with bracken and with the best views out to sea. They probably weren't really steps. They didn't really lead anywhere. But the rock's whimsical shape led you to think someone *had* bothered to dig them out. In the full flush of my recent re-reading of the novel, I sat down and remembered passages from its pages. I thought how the concerns of those young ragamuffins who spent their afternoons there weren't any different to mine. The only difference was that they dreamt and watched liners setting out to the Americas, while I had to be content with the Trans-Mediterranean Company ferries heading to Majorca.

Following the plan I'd mapped out, I took a dozen photos with my mobile, so the steps could be seen in context, before I started to go down. I was excited that I'd accomplished my objective, and was now anticipating the next challenge I'd set myself, namely, to make my descent to a specific spot in the city centre following an imaginary straight line. This mountain to sea route was a delightfully Barcelona thing and ideal for a re-discovery like mine. It meant following the natural course of the streams that gave their names to a number of streets and the natural path followed by locals from those areas when they went down to eat paella on the beach, the usual direction for demonstrations in revolutionary times or the underground channels of sewers whose rivers of shit flowed into the sea.

I cheated a bit. Rather than follow a straight line that would have taken me to Passeig de Sant Joan, I turned off towards Gràcia. It was part of my plan for a fresh immersion in the novel. The three youngsters lived in a street in the neighbourhood that was perpendicular to the coast. I walked down it and registered one detail: if the story described a single bar in a ten-block stretch, there were now twenty or so, and most offered some kind of exotic cuisine. The scenario was barely recognizable. The exact place where the hero lived, the boy who wanted to control the world, was now a supermarket chain. And there was no trace of the tram tracks. But I wasn't disappointed. That photo of the three steps on the Montaña Pelada was now a treasure safely stored in the virtual folder of my mobile. That undeniable piece of evidence was what I most prized. In its way, the photo preserved the vantage point of the broken dreams of generations of Barcelona youngsters, the real throne of dispossessed children. That writer had captured on paper the melancholy that had so often overwhelmed me up there.

I walked along gripping the mobile in my trouser pocket and staring at the to-and-fro of books and roses. In a couple of hours walking in the centre would be a real headache.

Luckily, the queue wasn't too long. The writers had only set up behind parapets of books a few minutes ago. Some were busy talking among themselves. Barely twenty readers were queueing in front of mine. Most carried his last title for him to sign. Others, some of his old books. And one couple was carrying nothing at all. Perhaps they just wanted a photo with him. I was afraid that would put him in a bad mood. In fact, it was the first time in many years that he'd agreed to sign copies on the day of Sant Jordi. Perhaps it was because he was tired of saying no to his publishers. Or because he felt happier about this novel than previous ones.

In any case, I was sure he'd not be keen to be in any selfie. He wasn't the right age and it wasn't his style. If somebody suggested it, there was the risk he would be annoyed and abandon the lot of us. Quite right too.

I didn't even want to look. In fact, as I progressed, I was only guided by the elegant sashays of the girl in front of me in the queue, her long legs funnelled into tight black jeans. Though I did stare into the writer's eyes when it was her turn. He looked her up and down, discreetly, not lingering, or so I thought. Frankly, my only worry was what I should say to him. I wanted to find the right words.

He dispatched the girl in a minute and then directed his weary gaze at me. Next one. That was the message from his sleepy eyes.

My hands were sweating when I showed him the screen of my mobile with the photo of the mythical steps dug out from the limestone in the Guinardó.

'That's them, right?' I burbled.

'What's that?' he asked as he peered rather bad-temperedly over the top of his glasses, leaning towards my telephone to see better.

'The steps, the steps on the Montaña Pelada where your three characters sit every afternoon.'

I relived the scene minutes later, as I headed up Passeig de Gràcia looking for the entrance to the metro, and feeling quite ruffled. He had grabbed the book I was holding under my arm and opened it at the title page in an amazingly deft fashion, already quite oblivious to the photo I was showing him.

'To whom should I dedicate it?'

'To my girlfriend, Elisabet.'

'In Catalan or Spanish?'

I watched the unsteady hand of someone who had stopped using a pen many years ago. I think he responded to my question when he added the date under his signature.

'It's not real, everything is invented, including the steps. It's a novel.'

I didn't have a girlfriend, or know any Elisabet, although I've always liked the name. I loved it when it was pronounced in Catalan, with the emphasis on the fourth syllable, and not the second, as in English. Like: ElisaBET. With the sibilant 's' of a Romance language. While I waited for him to give me my copy back, I noticed that the writer's rushed inscription had taken a victim. At least, initially. The 'a' of Elisabet was conspicuously absent between the 's' and the 'b'. Hey, the day had only just begun, yet he was already conserving energy when he signed my book, I reflected. However, after he'd finished, in a gesture that commanded respect, he retraced his steps and punctiliously inserted the missing vowel. A wonderfully italicized 'a'.

Dead Time

Teresa Solana

Before Soledad's alarm clock rings, she slips out of bed and tiptoes out of the bedroom so as not to alert her husband. She's been pretending to sleep for hours, stifling the need to move or change position, curled and still as she watches the hands of the clock slowly advance and waits for the minute hand to give her permission to escape from a bed she and Ramon have shared for almost thirty years. Only a few months ago, when that irritating ring went off compelling her to get up at five-thirty a.m., Soledad enjoyed snatching five more minutes of comforting warmth from the sheets and idly lingering, but ever since she's been so restless, she doesn't even wait for the alarm. Ramon knows that Soledad has never liked being an early riser, beginning the day before the first glimmer of dawn, and he'd be surprised to discover that recently she's been getting up so early. Fortunately, a couple of days each week, Ramon has to leave home when it's still dark to go to Mercabarna and then Soledad falls into a precarious sleep that brings no relief and leaves her even more exhausted. Ramon doesn't realize that for a good number of weeks, as soon as Soledad shuts her eyes, she is troubled by one nightmare after another.

In the kitchen, in silence and almost the pitch-black, Soledad makes coffee and nibbles a madeleine before swallowing a tranquillizer. She's not hungry, but decides to ignore her stomach's queasy protests and forces herself to finish her frugal breakfast. She's lost ten kilos in next-to-no time and is alone among her friends in being able to boast she still wears a size thirty-eight, though her bones are starting to stick out and she knows the excuse she is on a diet to keep her figure soon won't convince a soul. Her skinny body, the purple rings framing her grey eyes, will soon betray her and she's even more terrified by the idea that Ramon will find out that she's being worn down by fear. When she's in the bathroom and making an effort not to vomit the coffee and madeleine it was such a struggle to consume, she promises herself she will eat a filled roll in the middle of the morning and drink one of those sickly sweet juices she's always spurned. Perhaps she's got it all wrong, she tells herself unconvincingly, perhaps her suspicions are only a ridiculous misunderstanding. Innocent coincidences she has misread that have other explanations.

A year ago the city was devastated by the discovery of twelve corpses in the basements of the Ninot Market, in the Eixample: the bodies of twelve women who had been raped, beaten, stuffed in industrial black plastic sacks, and abandoned in one of the storerooms in the entrails of that building. That macabre find upset everyone—so many bodies packed into such a small space—though it was particularly disturbing for those who work and shop in the market, generally women who still resist the lure of big supermarkets and prefer the bustle of the stalls, the everyday chit-chat with stallholders, the mix of aromas from fresh greens, fresh fruit, cooked vegetables, spices, different kinds of meat and fish, sharp smells that fuse in haphazard ways and give the market its characteristic tang, almost from another era, the only thing that doesn't change in this precinct that has now decided to modernize and that for the moment occupies a space opposite the Hospital Clínico while the original wrought-iron structure on Carrer Mallorca is refurbished.

The autopsies revealed that the oldest of the corpses had suffered thirty years of oblivion; the most recent had been there only twelve months. They were all young women, aged between sixteen and twenty-five, and prostitutes judging by the shabby rags and wigs adorning their skeletons.

Nobody had missed them, and if it hadn't been for the modernizing of the building, they'd probably still be rotting down there and no one would have been any the wiser about their presence below the market's hustle and bustle. Their grave, a small storeroom, protected by a rusty padlock, was hidden behind metal panels and nobody knew who it belonged to. Most of those working in the market weren't aware of its existence, and those who did realize it was there at some point had forgotten all about that tiny room where building workers reconstructing the foundations discovered those bodies in different phases of decomposition. Nothing strange about that, employees come and go; stalls change owners. Some, that don't seem to attract customers, are constantly changing hands; others are sold after their owners retire, and only a few are passed on from parents to children and can boast of a hundred years of continuity. Unlike other markets on the outskirts, the ones languishing from the tempting prices offered by big supermarket chains, the Ninot, in the heart of the left side of the Eixample, has never ceased to be the heart of that bourgeois neighbourhood where common-sense grid-iron streets coexist with the flamboyance of surreal modernist façades, a marine horizon, and the silhouette of the mountain. The queues lining up every day by the stalls are a mix of social classes and passports, trades and languages, something that is true of most of the districts in this city whose mestizo vocation and diversity of accents seems endless. A city, Barcelona, friendly at times, prickly at others, open, surprising, and suspicious. And for a year a city that has been shocked by bodies that point to an unpunished murderer who is adopting the guise of an upstanding citizen.

The first time she saw that box she'd only been married to Ramon for a few months. It was a chance find, when she decided to spring clean the room her husband had set up to keep all the paperwork generated by the butcher's his parents had owned for forty years in the Ninot. Ramon had asked Soledad to leave the room in peace, to forget about cleaning it—'papers don't gather dirt and easily get into a mess'—but Soledad, brought up with an ancestral horror of insects in the home, went in now and then on the sly, removed cobwebs and washed the floor down with bleach and water. Their dingy but spacious flat was located in one of those old blocks on Carrer Casanova, a few minutes from the market, and had been a present from Ramon's parents. Born in a more modest house in the working-class district of Santa Coloma, Soledad was used to the shenanigans and noise that came with living with three brothers who shared a bedroom, and was scared stiff when she was left alone among so many empty rooms, especially when she had to walk along that long gloomy passage that acted like a backbone stiffening the disposition of the rooms and uniting the two ends of their home.

At that time, when Ramon was away, Soledad tried to keep herself busy in order to fight off the depression that overwhelmed her when she was by herself. Something that usually happened on Sundays, when Ramon went down to the bar after lunch to play cards and watch football. It was on one of those interminable afternoons when her anxiety threatened to turn to despair that Soledad decided the office needed a good clean and went in set on getting rid of the grime piling up everywhere. The room overlooked an inner yard where neighbours hung out their washing and had a window that was never opened and which let in very little light. The stale, sticky air within its four walls stank of another era and the black tobacco cigarettes Ramon smoked.

Soledad had been cleaning for a while when she came across the box almost by accident. It was an ordinary brown shoebox apparently just hidden by a pile of yellowing papers. Soledad wouldn't even have noticed it if she hadn't opened the metal filing cabinet where Ramon kept their passports and important documents, hoping to put an end to the silver fish that were having a field day in its various drawers. Although it seemed out of place, Soledad thought Ramon must use the box to keep together receipts or invoices and made nothing of it.

The box weighed very little and, initially, Soledad thought it was empty. However, when she put it on the table, she noticed something slide inside and curiosity led her to open it. It contained a cheap, tacky bracelet, a rusty brass necklace encrusted with imitation plastic precious stones—junk. She shut it, didn't give it another thought and pursued the silver fish. When she'd finished cleaning, wintry darkness filled the sky and a thin, rickety moon was beginning to glimmer behind the windows of a wooden gallery from where on a bright day she sometimes caught a glimpse of the sea.

That evening the game finished late and Ramon didn't return home until past midnight. Soledad had to wait to the following day to tell him she'd spruced up his room, and that she had accidentally found that necklace. Ramon lost his temper when he heard that Soledad had dared to rummage among his things, and insults quickly turned to screams and accusations. Soledad was upset by Ramon's furious reaction and burst into tears. At most she had expected an affectionate rebuff, but never an outburst of frenzied indignation she felt was unwarranted. When Ramon finally calmed down, he told her he didn't know who the necklace belonged to, that he'd found it in the market a long time ago, and kept it in case a customer mentioned she'd lost it. It had never occurred to Soledad to ask him to justify the possession of that bauble; she thought his explanation was reasonable enough and assumed the subject was closed. Ramon apologized for bawling at her, perhaps he had gone too far, and Soledad, relieved to hear her husband's *mea culpa*, accepted his excuses and asked him to forgive her.

From that day on Soledad never went back into the office the door to which, in any case, Ramon had quickly padlocked. He justified that by saying he kept cash there and didn't trust Mari, the girl who cleaned their flat. Soledad thought Ramon's desire to keep her out of his office must be because he perhaps used it to hide some of the pornographic magazines with which Spain in the nineteen-eighties was trying to recover from forty years of sexual repression enforced by the dictatorship. She felt that was ridiculous, but as she couldn't but be curious, now and then she looked around the flat hoping to find the key to that padlock. She never did, because Ramon always took his keys with him and she never dared ask for it and trigger another of those rows.

The door remained shut, and, over time, Soledad got used to the huge size of that flat and coexistence with a room that was locked tight. Until early one morning, a car going at top speed jumped the lights and crashed into Ramon's van, an accident that unexpectedly put those office keys into her hands.

Ramon had been on his way back from the slaughter-house with his transit packed with meat and didn't even see the vehicle coming. He was lucky, but the crash broke the bones in his shoulder and they had to take him to hospital.

In a haze because of the collision and painkillers, he called Soledad and told her he'd had an accident. Soledad, who'd just got out of bed, quickly dressed and rushed to the hospital.

Ramon's injuries came down to a number of bruises and a broken shoulder, there were lots of patients waiting in emergencies, and he wouldn't be discharged for some time. Ramon had left the car insurance documents in his office, and, as he had to fill in an accident report sheet, he handed Soledad his keys and asked her to fetch the papers.

She hadn't been inside that space for fifteen years, and, as she went in, she felt she had every right to peer around. She spent a while checking the contents of the desk drawers and the shelves, opened boxes and folders, and found nothing noteworthy. To get into the metal filing cabinet where she had left the shoebox that was the cause of their first quarrel as a married couple, she had to look for the small key to the lock on Ramon's key ring.

The yellowing papers had gone, but the shoebox was in the same place. Soledad retrieved it from the cabinet, took the lid off and saw that, in addition to the necklace she'd seen years ago, there was a fake red leather belt, a black garter with pink bows, some false eyelashes, and gaudy gold earrings. That find upset her, especially because she recognized their erotic nature and, after placing them on the table, she gazed at them in amazement while she tried to find a plausible excuse for their presence in Ramon's office.

It was obvious they didn't belong to any customer, they weren't lost property Ramon had happened to find by his stall; there had to be another explanation. Soledad had guessed some time ago that there were other women in Ramon's life—she'd noticed the smell of other women on his underwear—and that motley collection of feminine objects only confirmed her suspicions. However, when she examined them with an expert purchaser's eye and recognized their scant value, Soledad realized they belonged to cut-price prostitutes who must have given Ramon the kind of vulgar pleasures she refused him when they were making love. Relieved to think that the women Ramon was deceiving her with weren't lovers on the make, the kind who represented competition, Soledad returned the box back to its place, locked the office door, and left the flat.

On her way back to the hospital she stopped by at a locksmith's and had a copy of the keys made, which she hid in a packet of tissues she was carrying in her bag. Over the next few days, while Ramon was at home recovering from the accident, Soledad weighed up the pros and cons of throwing her discovery in his face and asking him to explain his behaviour, but she concluded her husband's sex-on-the-side was no threat to her marriage and that the reproaches she was contemplating might have unforeseen consequences, so she opted to say nothing. Soledad still remembered her poverty-stricken childhood, the poor food and second-hand clothes, and still felt lucky she enjoyed that comfortable life free of money worries she shared with Ramon.

In the end, she told herself as a kind of pitiful consolation that her husband wasn't the first or only man who paid for sex to make up for lack of fun in the conjugal bed.

'Soledad, are you feeling OK?'

The question was asked by Vero, who had helped on the stall ever since Ramon's mother retired. Soledad is slicing off steaks and making an effort to smile at their customers, but she's been out-of-sorts for months and Vero is afraid she will cut herself again. Soledad still has the stitches in her left hand from a few days ago, when she almost lost the distal phalanx of her ring finger, and the big bandage, lack of sleep, and tranquillizer she took before leaving home means her hand moves awkwardly. Vero thinks Soledad is depressed because she's menopausal and can't get used to the idea that she will never have children—they've talked about that more than once—but as Soledad is very reserved and her boss to boot, Vero prefers to say nothing. Although they get on well, they aren't friends, and Vero doesn't want to risk Soledad taking her comments badly—she might sack her and take on an apprentice prepared to accept half her pay with the excuse of the crisis.

Vero's looking ridiculous today. She has gathered up her hair in two high bunches and squeezed her forty-five years and eighty kilos into her daughter's school uniform. She's wearing long socks, a short skirt, a white blouse stained with fake blood and smeared her face bright green: she is a school-girl zombie. Next to her, in a black dress that highlights how skinny she is, with a wig with grey strands, a pallid face, and crimson red lips, Soledad is doing her to best to look like Frankenstein's bride. It is the eve of All Saints Day, and market-traders have donned disguises to match the macabre decorations on their stalls in an attempt to attract attention and new customers. There are lots of pumpkins and skeletons, people from beyond the grave, and monstrous caricatures. A cheerful, festive Halloween has for some time been gaining ground on the traditional sweet potatoes, chestnuts, and *panellets* made from marzipan and pine nuts, and this year, for the first time, the traders of the Ninot have decided to defy tradition and join in the vogue for disguises. People like to make fun of death, if only for a day, and wreak revenge on the horror provoked by the monsters they see at the cinema.

Vero looks at Soledad on the sly and sees it is an effort for her boss to smile and chat with customers who are discussing the decorations and praising her disguise. For months

Soledad has been struggling to come to work, the Ninot is no longer that welcoming place where everyone knows her, and she never feels alone. Although she still goes to their stall every day, she has tried to hide the entangled thoughts crowding her brain.

What Vero doesn't know is that the listless apathy she senses in Soledad's state of mind began the day she discovered that the twelve women found in the basements of the old Ninot market were prostitutes nobody had missed. That same morning, after pretending she had a migraine so she could escape from the butcher's, she went home and went into the office intending to take a look at the old shoebox and count the objects it contained. Ever since she'd had a copy of the keys, Soledad periodically went into the office and checked on the box that over the years had been filling up with new trashy trifles. That day, when she opened the filing cabinet, the box had gone, and she felt scared.

Soledad scoured the flat looking for the box, but couldn't find it. For some reason, Ramon had decided to get rid of it or had hidden it elsewhere. She began to think Ramon might be the murderer the police were after. What if the objects in that shoebox weren't fetishes belonging to the prostitutes Ramon bedded, as she had thought, but grim trophies snatched from the victims discovered in El Ninot?

* * *

Aurora Ballester, deputy-inspector in the *mossos d'esquadra*, downed her second coffee of the morning as she scrutinized the photo puzzle now dominating her office in the police station in Les Corts. A total of one hundred and thirty-six snapshots form a perfect rectangle on the cork noticeboard. The photos correspond to the faces of seventeen middle-aged women in a row, and each face spawns a column of eight different images of that same face. The photos on the top row go back seven months and are the oldest; the ones Ballester pinned up only minutes ago on the lower half of the board carry yesterday's date.

When they asked her to take charge of the investigation, Ballester immediately understood that the shortcuts of forensic science and its microscopic subtleties would be of little use in the case of the Ninot murderer. Most of the corpses were ancient, there were no fingerprints on the plastic bags, and the aggressor's DNA on the bodies wouldn't have survived their physical deterioration. There were no witnesses or dates to help check alibis, and the painstaking searches of suspects' houses had brought no conclusive evidence. After two months of enquiries and energy-sapping interrogations the deputy-inspector's team was beginning to lose heart and steam, and, bogged down by a lack of solid clues, their investigations risked grinding to a halt.

It was Ballester who'd had the idea of the photos. Their police work had managed to establish a profile and reduce the number of suspects to seventeen, and Ballester decided that if the evidence she had to hand didn't allow them to identify the murderer, it was necessary to change their strategy and find a reluctant witness to help them solve the case. The faces Ballester has been pinning to the cork board for seven months belonged to the wives of the suspects, and although she's questioned them several times without achieving a confession or quiet hint, Ballester isn't giving up. She knows from experience that one of those seventeen women is living trapped within the dead time of suspicion and she's confident that sooner or later the woman's restraint will give way.

Ballester looks at the last row of photos and notices one face that seems to have aged more quickly than the rest and reaches for her magnifying glass. Ballester compares this face to previous ones, checks the name and data of the woman whose face is on the snapshot, and decides that she will go to the market that morning and pay her a visit.

Everyone in the market knows the *mossos* are working on the hypothesis that the murderer is a single individual, a man who is forty-five plus and has been connected to the market for at least thirty years. Soledad doesn't know what to do. She doesn't want to go to the police without first speaking to Ramon, but doesn't dare confront him, and she is embarrassed by that. If she is right and Ramon is the psychopath the newspapers are talking about, how will he react if she asks after the shoebox and its contents? Will he attack her and beat her to death, as he had done to those poor women? And if she reveals her suspicions to the *mossos* and it turns out she's got it wrong, how will Ramon ever forgive her?

Ever since she suspected that Ramon is the Ninot murderer, Soledad has been repeatedly wondering why he decided to marry her of all the girls that worked in the market. A rather shy, not particularly pretty girl who was honest and hardworking, but from a much lower social class than most girls Ramon was seeing at the time. They'd met in the market, and, despite her timidity and gauche ways, Ramon noticed her and asked her out.

Soledad doesn't understand what Ramon saw in her and the explanation she feels intuitively is devastating. Soledad can see herself washing up in the kitchen in that tiny flat in Santa Coloma, keeping down the tears while she tries to remove the bloodstains from her father's police uniform as he boasts about how good he is at inflicting pain on the detained who are sent to the station on Via Layetana for questioning. The portrait of the Generalísimo and the Spanish flag are witness to her father's coarse laughter, and while he drinks his after-dinner coffee, he mercilessly mocks the pleas of the wretches he tortures with impunity in the station cellars. That coarse laughter, made even cruder by his intake of tobacco and anisette, has stayed with Soledad for ever, and the cowardly silence she sustained then, and which descended over her when she discovered Ramon was consorting with prostitutes, now seem of a piece, the answer to all her questions.

Ballester doesn't cook. Perhaps that's why she'd never been to the Ninot Market before taking this case on. Like everyone else she was intrigued by its name, and soon discovered it went back to the days when it was a street market and the traders set up their stalls on the Carrers Valencia, Mallorca, and Villarroel. In those days there was an inn with something of a reputation on Valencia that displayed a *ninot* on its façade. The innkeeper's daughter, who was betrothed to a young man who lived in the Barceloneta, used to walk down to the port area to visit her fiancé, and on one visit she'd watched a boat being broken up and had fallen in love with the vessel's figurehead, a chubby cabin boy holding his sailor's cap and diploma from nautical school. The girl managed to retrieve it, and when she took it home, her father placed it on the doorstep of his inn. The establishment soon began to be called 'the cabin boy's inn', and, by extension, the stalls set up around the tavern appropriated the name and over time the whole market adopted the name of *El mercat del Ninot*—'The Cabin-Boy's Market'. When the building on Carrer Mallorca was inaugurated in 1894, town-hall politicians baptized it with the official name of *El Mercado del Porvenir*, 'The Market of the Future', but thirty years later the Republic put that right, and restored its popular name, the one people had continued to use. In their anti-republican fury, the Francoist dictatorship re-baptized it *El Mercado del Porvenir*, but the name never caught on, and the new democracy restored the name locals from the neighbourhood had given it a hundred years before.

Ballester doesn't realize it is Halloween, and when she walks into the market, she is surprised to find most of the traders are wearing disguises and that the stalls are decorated with numerous skeletons and dozens of pumpkins. As she closes in on the butchers where Soledad works and recognizes her behind her disguise, she understands how the character adopted by the woman she's come to question is an omen that confirms her intuition and she feels her heart beat more quickly. From behind the counter, Soledad notices the deputy-inspector approach looking very agitated and, when she looks her in the eye, she realizes that she *knows* and bursts into tears.

And suddenly Soledad feels light, as if she'd being transported by invisible wings, and, to Vero's amazement, she removes her apron and wig, leaves the stall and walks towards Ballester, whom she tells about a shoebox behind a padlocked door.

G.METRO
CUARTELILLO

The Shoeshine and La Locomotora

Alfredo Bryce Echenique

It was a big effort for Peruvian Eleodoro Holguín, who'd spent a lifetime in Europe, to order the cities and countries where he'd lived chronologically and he was always amused when Spaniards or people in Madrid often referred to a traditional shoeshine as *un limpia*, a cleaner. What's more, when he heard that word, he'd often recall the shoeshine stall in the centre of Lima, blessed with the catchy tag of the Chammy Magicians, where he trooped manically every morning of his youth until he departed for Europe. It was close to the rambling old pile of San Marcos, in the University Park, in three faculties of which he had begun but never finished three degree courses. What he liked about the 'Four Centuries', as it was pompously referred to, was the varied character of its courtyards where there were as many students from Lima as from the provinces, who often came from places Eleodoro had never heard of, and he never bothered to ask about them, as he knew he'd very likely never hear of them again: the moment he left San Marcos, without any kind of certificate, he would set sail for Europe. And what was he intending to do in Europe? Really, he didn't have a clue, apart from practising the languages he had studied so intensively, since he read any book that fell into his hands in a frenzy, particularly history books and novels, though he harboured a deep distrust of translations.

Besides, his decision to journey to Europe had been a hundred per cent the consequence of a phrase, as absurd as it was redundant, that he heard someone say one day, quite by chance, on a bus; it was uttered by a guy who was dead set on heading to the Old Continent, and the friend he was sharing a seat with asked why.

'A journey to Europe is the fundamental step a man must take in life,' came the idiot's lofty, platitudinous response.

But the truth is that a few months later, with hardly any money and even less clothing, especially the winter kind, though obviously, with a spectacular selection of spotless shoes, which had recently revisited the artistic hands of the Chammy Magicians, so he wouldn't need to rush to find a good shoeshine stall after landing on the other side of the pond, Eleodoro Holguín landed in Paris. Naturally before he went, there were tearful farewells, exuberant embraces, and everybody wished him great success and a prompt return to his native patch, as if both would be simultaneous and rapid. Laconic as ever, Eleodoro Holguín responded a thousand and one times to drunken accusations that his departure from a Peru that needed him showed a lack of patriotism, and then, almost as if he *were* a renowned leader, he responded with the lofty words he'd overheard on that bus, although with much more passion, uniquely and exclusively nourished, of course, by the amount he had imbibed.

'Goodbye, youngsters, lifelong friends, beloved fans from those historic days . . . ,' began Eleodoro.

But then he was accused of being a traitor to the fatherland, because he made his farewells with tangos and not local waltzes from Lima, though he immediately put things straight by repeating that he was only going to Europe, dear friends, because a journey to Europe is a necessary step in the life of any man. The immediate effect of those words, to his very last night in Peru, was to produce tears, admiration, total silence, and unbridled devotion. So, naturally, he managed to leave peacefully, if with a long, long list of everything, without which, he would find life practically impossible in Europe, starting with stone-bass *ceviche* and ice-cold beer.

Of course, none of that was true, though what did begin to drive Eleodoro Holguín—the shiny shoe maniac—crazy was the absence or almost non-existence of shoeshines. And he tried everything, even mutual shoe-polishing, on a bench, three times a week, with a very nice compatriot, but this frequency rate, or lack of such, meant very little, particularly if one takes into account the downpours and drizzles, the crunchy snow and sleet, the thunder claps unleashing furious sheets of rain, and the horrible poo left by the nasty yapping little dogs that so abound in Paris, all mixed up with the grit they occasionally threw on pavements to ensure people didn't slip. In the end, it was the city itself that was dirtying Eleodoro's life and shoes even though he had found two new compatriots for two mutual shoe-polishing sessions a week, which meant he now had the seven days covered, but he soon realized that wasn't enough in Paris where one strolls so much. And as he always carried three chammy cloths and two little brushes in his pockets, he soon earned the nickname of the Shoe Loony and became the butt of everyone's laughter. And, what's more, girls, who in Peru had always praised his spotlessly shiny shoes, now avoided him like the plague the second he started to tell them one can't clean one's own shoes properly, since the first step is to unlace them completely, hold them up at a proper height, which was a hundred per cent necessary to have a properly clear view of all four sides, even if, at first sight, they only seemed to have three . . .

Paris finally defeated him, as in turn did Montpellier, Marseille, Nantes, Orléans, and Rouen, and he had awful setbacks in Germany, Austria, Belgium, Holland, Ireland, and England, countries he abandoned after very short stays—in rainy Ireland, for example, he barely lasted a week—not to mention the Nordic countries, icy, rainy Sweden, Norway, and Finland, which he fled like the devil. And, of course, he couldn't go to Spain, because he hadn't come to Europe to forget the languages he'd studied so intensely in Lima, rather he'd gone there to practise and learn them as well as he could, so he could read everything in their original language, since there was nothing he detested more than translations. Frankly, he loathed them, however good they were, almost as much as he loathed dirty shoes.

He finally threw in the sponge the day he bumped into a fellow in Milan airport who'd just landed from Madrid, and wore shoes with such a sheen Eleodoro Holguín had to give him the third degree, a vicious one at that, as to the origins of that splendid sheen.

'Glorieta de Bilbao, Madrid,' the guy snarled uneasily.

'So it's got a shoeshine stand with three or four chairs with proper arms and everything, right?'

'Well, there are three shoeshines, each with a chair and box of polish, and that's your lot.'

'And that's your lot?' asked Eleodoro Holguín, looking so disgruntled that the Spaniard, at the end of his tether, while pitying this cretin, added: 'But stay clear of the deaf-mute, because he is one hell of a bastard.'

'Which of the other two do you recommend, sir?'

'Damn me, what an idiot!' exclaimed the Spaniard, raising his arm threateningly and striding off.

Three days later, putting his shoes before his languages, Eleodoro Holguín installed himself in Madrid, where at ten sharp daily, he turned up in the Glorieta de Bilbao, and kept well clear of the loathsome, irritable, deaf-mute shoeshine. And he chose the Galician from the remaining two, as he was much more thorough than his rather insipid colleague from Extremadura. Otherwise, he always sought out work as a night-time receptionist in a cheap hotel. That was the ideal job for him, because of the few people coming in and out at night, and the almost total silence that meant he could fully devote himself to reading. Eleodoro had now been in Europe for over twenty years and had always had the same kind of work, attracted by that prolonged peace, and because guests came from very different countries and spoke numerous languages that he continued to study and needed to practise.

Eleodoro soon discovered that millions of tourists came to Spain, especially in summer, and that most headed to the beaches or the south, particularly, to Andalusia. So he took a trip there, and Sevilla, apart from its many other charms, seemed like the world centre for shoeshines. He opted to stay awhile, as usual as a night-time receptionist in a cheap hotel, but after two years he found he'd not really adapted to the city; he reckoned it was too casual and over-the-top for his character. A shoe polish had always been an endless source of pleasure, but every shoeshine in Sevilla tried to charge far too much and he had to spend the whole time haggling, until he thought enough is enough, which coincided with a call from a friend to say that a hotel in Barcelona, the quiet kind he liked, was seeking a night-time receptionist and paid really well.

Within days Eleodoro was in Barcelona and complaining to his friend that, apart from Las Ramblas, which had a Peruvian shoeshine who was a real nightmare, down to his patriotic, nostalgic patter, and use of the worst polishes and antediluvian chammies and brushes, he was finding it hard to find a decent shoeshine. What's more, he lived in Floridablanca, a street near Plaza España, and the other two shoeshines he knew were in Calles Mandri and Caspe, respectively, that is, quite a way from his hotel. Eleodoro Holguín was beginning to age, and found those long walks increasingly exhausting, and, naturally, he'd given up on the metro years ago because it was the ideal place for people to tread on your beautiful, shiny shoes and destroy their sheen.

But one day when Eleodoro was having a coffee in a bar in La Locomotora, a bar on the corner of Gran Via and Conde de Urgell, all of a sudden a shoeshine walked wearily in, whose accent could have been Argentinian or Uruguayan in his youth, or before his true nationality had been eroded by the passage of time. For the first time in his life, Eleodoro Holguín felt sorry for a shoeshine, since he normally felt that a man who exercised that profession, and did so well, was worthy of the greatest respect and admiration. And, from the distant days of the Chammy Magicians, respect and admiration, combined with a fatal attraction to those charged with keeping our shoes spotless and shiny, had always been the mark of his character, such that now he was astonished to find that this old, fat, bovine, down-at-heel shoeshine inspired real pity. And Eleodoro cursed, because the guy was the worst shoeshine ever and polished while drinking coffee or smoking a cigarette, and because either he never breathed out or it was eternally going out, he was always interrupting his polishing to light up. Moreover, his tins of polish were almost always practically empty, and the residues he used, more to maintain a pretence of cleaning than actually cleaning, were also completely dried out. Worst of all, as the guy seemed about to leave this world and no longer even pretended to clean, he expected you to pay for his expresso and that peculiar, yellow cigarette that lasted him the whole day. They were always chasing him out of La Locomotora, a cafeteria and restaurant with certain pretensions, though honestly it was a shabby, gloomy, depressing place. Nevertheless, the poor guy always reappeared twice a day as if nothing had happened, at around 11 a.m. and 7 p.m., increasingly pathetic and removed from the real world.

So Eleodoro also began to reappear at La Locomotora, a.m. and p.m., in pursuit of that poor, faintly Argentinian shine, dragged there no doubt by the immense pity inspired by a man who embarks on the adventure of emigrating to Europe and ends up polishing shoes on street corners. What's more, as Eleodoro's hotel was close to La Locomotora, he was constantly bumping into him in the neighbourhood when he would reflect how that poor guy only possessed two or three almost empty polish tins and a few practically bald brushes to save himself from begging.

And when he least expected it, Eleodoro Holguín, who was about the same age as that pathetic shoeshine, found himself having four polishes a day, twice in the morning and twice in the afternoon. It was obvious why, or at least he thought it was: every morning and evening he cleaned his shoes with that poor old Argentinian or Uruguayan, who dirtied rather than cleaned his shoes, and then he would get them cleaned twice in Calle Caspe, a prudent distance away, so they were left just as he wanted them, once again.

And the only other change was that eventually La Locomotora shut down for good and that poor fellow now ruined his shoes on the terrace of a café by the name of Ordesa, which was also on the Gran Via, but on the opposite pavement, and when he'd painfully threaded his way across the three lanes and pavements of this boulevard, in a striking imitation of a weary ox, he would dally for hours outside the derelict Locomotora.

Neighbours

Jordi Nopca

Jia came to Barcelona seven years ago. He's worked hard all this time to achieve the goal that had lured him from China so soon after his twenty-sixth birthday: to run his own bar. Nothing's been easy. He's had to face various new challenges. Meeting his future wife, Liang. Moving house from Sants to the Eixample, learning Spanish and a little Catalan, more ably than most of his compatriots, while working in emporia that reeked of plastic, and doing overtime in bakeries that also served coffee and sold demijohns of mineral water they set out in neat, straight lines like gravestones in a cemetery. Jia had finally been able to save enough money to advance six months' rent on the bar in the entrance to the Filmoteca at 33, Avinguda de Sarrià.

Several times a day Jia reminds himself that he is a lucky man: when he's dealing with a customer, or is bored and waiting for someone to drop in the bar mid-morning, or is preparing a cold ham roll with a look of distaste on his face. However busy the day's been, late on he still has to carry out the mandatory routine inspection of the bathroom, reflecting as ever that somebody had splashed it around with annoying thoroughness and creative talent. Even then he never forgets that he is a lucky man.

Things are going well. He feels happy with his enterprise and proud that Liang is at his side: they spend most of the day behind the bar, a space with a symbolic value in their relationship that goes way beyond the marriage bed. Their life could be an example of exemplary self-improvement and admirable tenacity. A model the political class could use to embellish their speeches and statistics on the subject of *newcomers*. The couple could have a spot on a television series about world cuisine and wax lyrical about the delicious Cantonese dishes they cook and consume in their bar while their customers contemplate a flat white, a beer, or a tapa of *patates braves*. Conversely, arthouse film buffs linger by the window watching them eat, as they stand in the ticket queue, and nostalgically remember Asian highlights that have bewitched them as voracious fans of celluloid: Kim Ki-duk, Tsai Ming-Liang, Chen Kaige, and Zhang Yimou.

Jia and Liang's model behaviour, worthy of the widest praise—even in the most right-on of literary vignettes—is of no use at all when the lady with the filthy hair and fingernails walks into their bar as she has done for the last six weeks. Her visits are always unpredictable and shot through with the sick delirium that can erupt in a dream and ruin a peaceful night. They've never caught her entering the bar: they always find her sitting on a chair, head slumped over the table, as if it were a bottle someone had knocked over and needed only the lightest breeze to roll it on the floor and shatter it to smithereens.

The first time Jia tapped the none-too-salubrious brown coat wrapped round her shoulders, when she opened her eyes, he asked if she was feeling well.

'Gin and tonic,' came the reply.

It was eight o'clock on a Saturday night. Jia brought her the drink that she knocked back in two nervous gulps the second he put it on the table. Her head immediately slumped back on the table: she'd apparently fallen asleep. A few minutes later, Liang went to get Jia who was in the bathroom by now. The woman had left without paying, she told him as he conscientiously scoured a sink.

Days later the stranger reappeared in the same brown coat—slightly grimier than on her first visit—and an identically leaden head. She ordered another gin and tonic and Jia barely reacted. She mumbled a confused complaint, and after downing her drink, ordered another, and yet another, after she'd knocked back her second. Jia decided to allow her a third when he saw the woman's red, puffy hands were clutching a crumpled fifty-euro note.

On that occasion she paid for her drinks, though she spewed the lot up in the bathroom. Jia found her offering in the early evening and decided there and then that he wouldn't let the woman back in, but a week later her ruddy head was slumped on a table again. She seemed drunker than ever. Her purple-veined nose was streaming. Her open mouth displayed teeth as a yellow as a ten *cèntim* coin. A couple of students sitting nearby immediately asked for their bill and went to the cinematheque that was showing a cycle of Portuguese films with the latest films by Manoel de Oliveira, João César Monteiro, and João Canijo. Liang collected up the empty cups and when she walked back behind the bar, she told Jia that *her* smell was *intolerable*. They should throw her out. He went over but before he could utter a word, she opened one eye and said: 'Gin and tonic.'

Jia told her he couldn't serve her because they were about to shut the bar. The sun was still shining on some of the tables: it was barely half-past four. The woman struggled to her feet and said she was leaving.

She was back within days. It was mid-morning. A man in his seventies was at the bar; he sported huge paste spectacles covered in finger marks and a moustache like a clothes brush. A regular in the bar, he solved the Sudoku in all the papers he could get his hands on (Jia and Liang let him indulge his vice because he left big tips). The old fellow noticed the woman and snorted loudly, which caught Jia's attention. He now saw her and snorted as well, even though he usually tried to repress any expression of unease, especially in the presence of a customer.

'Do you know her?' the man asked in Spanish, and Jia mumbled a 'yes' that sounded more like 'I don't know what you're on about'.

Liang was washing up at the other end of the bar, and looked away from the sink for a couple of seconds, listening hard as she worked. The man said very little but enough for Jia to decide to go over to the woman and ask her if she was all right, after he'd tugged on her filthy brown coat.

'Gin and tonic,' came the reply.

Jia replied that they'd run out of gin and brought her a Coke which she greeted with a contemptuous snarl. She downed it in one gulp and fell asleep, her head slumped back on the table.

'What a soak,' the man said to Jia.

He was about to finish the Sudoku. That day it took him longer than usual, as he was intrigued to see whether or not they would kick that woman out of the bar. The waiter spoke to Liang in a language he couldn't decipher, but didn't seem set on going that far. The man skimmed the newspaper again before finally giving up: he went home not knowing how that situation sorted itself out.

Three or four weeks passed before Jia saw the woman again. It was one evening when he'd had to rush out to buy milk. It beggared belief but they were down to their last carton, and rather than wrangle with Liang about who was to blame for not upping the order from their supplier, he took off his apron, hung it up by the cash register, and said goodbye to his partner. Christmas lights, by the local prostitutes' red neon signs, dutifully heralded the news that Jesus's birth was nigh.

Jia found milk in the local supermarket and grabbed half a dozen cartons that would last them to the next morning. He had to join a lengthy queue to pay. He soon spotted their phantom customer: she was rummaging in her bag for money to buy the bottle of gin she wanted. Either she didn't have any or couldn't find any. People were griping at her, fed up with waiting for no good reason. Jia put the six pack of milk on the ground, patiently prepared to accept the delay. He was shocked when the woman, with a sudden burst of energy, tried to snatch the bottle from the hands of the girl on the till. She didn't get her way and was frogmarched out by a security guard who appeared from nowhere.

The queue shortened quickly as soon as the girl recovered from the shock. The fifty-year-old couple in front of Jia began muttering about the *drunkard*. They called her Rosa, as if they'd known her at some point. Perhaps they were neighbours, had been at tenants' meetings together, and been forced to jointly criticize the administrator's perpetual lack of efficiency. Perhaps they'd met in church on the occasional Sunday. Jia wrinkled his nose when he found himself imagining *that* possibility. He heard the couple mention the woman's son, by the name of Sergi, and whenever they mentioned his name they added 'poor boy', 'poor boy'—a repetition underlining the scale of the disaster—and exchanged plaintive glances as they said he'd been a such good student and nobody could have imagined him meeting such a sudden, *perplexing* end. That was all they said, and Jia stared at them, his curiosity aroused: he was about to ask for more details using the pretext that the old lady visited his bar now and then, but decided not to. And he later regretted that, because when he went back behind the bar, he could have stalled Liang's little telling-off—he'd taken too long to get back—by recourse to a strange, memorable story, of which, right now, he could only retail a couple of elements: that peculiar woman's son and the misfortune he had suffered.

A few days before Christmas, the Filmoteca was about to conclude a cycle of films directed by Raj Kapoor. It was advertising, as it did every year, a showing of *It's a Wonderful Life*, which Jia had seen on TV a few days after arriving in Barcelona, when he glutted himself on films to familiarize himself with his two new languages. All he could remember was that James Stewart played the main character. One lunchtime, when he was filling rolls, he felt he'd like to see it again and suggested to Liang that if there wasn't much happening the night it was showing, they might perhaps make an exception and close the bar early, buy a couple of tickets and pay for their first visit to the Filmoteca. She looked up from the tray where she was slicing potatoes, stared at him, and said they'd see it someday.

That same night, *that* woman reappeared. Jia found her sitting on a chair when he came back from stacking boxes in their storeroom. She was trying to keep her head up, and when she saw him, she waved in his direction.

'Gin and tonic,' she muttered when he was a few metres away.

Jia noticed a huge bloodstain on her coat. He asked her if she was all right, pointing rather hesitantly at the place where she might have sustained an injury. She laughed raucously and repeated her order: 'Gin and tonic.'

While he walked back behind the bar, the woman's head slumped on the table. It resounded loudly: an ominous sign. Jia grabbed his mobile and rang the police. The moment Liang heard her partner mention a bloodstain, she looked at the woman and saw a thick, dark pool of blood near her shabby shoes. They were the only three people in the bar, but before Jia could ring off, a small man with a shiny baldpate and inquisitive eyes walked in and sat on a stool by the bar.

'There's nothing we can do,' he told Liang, who had come over to ask what he wanted in his basic but understandable Catalan. 'She's a hopeless case. But don't worry: she'll get through the day.'

After that unexpected exchange, the man ordered a coffee, jumped down from his stool, went over to the woman, and said: '*Senyora* Rosa. Can you hear me? Listen, please!' he shook her a couple of times and managed to get her to lift her head. 'You've had enough for today. Off you go home now.'

'I only want a gin and tonic.'

'You know that's not on. You're covered in blood, *Senyora* Rosa. What happened? Did you have another fall?'

'I couldn't give a shit.'

'Listen. When I left the house, I thought I saw the neighbours by your door. I reckon they wanted another word with you.'

'The neighbours want another word with me? What do those women want now?'

Helped by the man, she clumsily got up from her chair. Astonished, Jia observed the scene. He even raised an arm to say goodbye to his customer. Both walked slowly along the bar and she left a small trail of blood behind her. The man hadn't touched his coffee that was still steaming on the counter, as the couple drifted away into the distance. Neither Jia nor Liang had it in them to do anything to stop them.

Ten minutes later two cops walked into their premises and found Jia and Liang sitting in silence at the table where the incident had taken place. Martínez the head cop quickly asked them to explain themselves. How come they'd let the woman get away? Had they ever seen that man who'd walked into their bar and *hypnotized* the local drunkard? Had they noticed whether she was carrying anything under her coat? What did they think had caused the wound? The cop's questions were so direct that Jia plucked up courage and asked him if he'd previously been aware of '*Senyora* Rosa'.

'Is there anyone around here who doesn't know her story?' retorted Martínez, as he extracted a packet of cigarettes from one of his uniform's multiple pockets, took out a cigarette, and lit up with a swagger.

Jia looked blank. The cop launched into the story of the woman and her son Sergi. They lived close to the Escola Industrial, five minutes from the bar. All alone. Nobody knew anything about the father: either there wasn't one, or he'd fled the scene so long ago nobody expected him to come back. Rosa worked as an accountant for a small hotel chain. The boy went to school. The years went by, as did the holidays. Two, six, nine years. The mother celebrated her fortieth birthday, and remained unattached. The boy went from elementary to high school. The mother began to dye her hair copper. Her son's face was covered in acne, he smoked his first cigarettes and tried marihuana. Both changes signalled that the youngster was bursting out of the childhood shell at a fast rate.

'Their lives were going more or less OK,' the cop summed up, 'until something horrible happened two Christmases ago. Sit tight, because I bet you've not heard many stories like theirs.'

Martínez, the cop in charge, took a few long drags on his cigarette and told Jia and Liang that one fine day *Senyora* Rosa discovered Sergi was hiding a pellet gun in the wardrobe. They had a big row that night: he said a friend had asked him to look after it for a few days and that he'd be returning the weapon soon enough. His mother insisted he got rid of it before the end of the week. If he didn't, he wouldn't get his monthly pocket money. Sergi barely whimpered at her threat and assured her he would give the gun back before Monday. He took note and got rid of it, or at least that's what Rosa thought until a few days later, when she was putting a load of clothes to wash, she found traces of blood on her son's underpants. When she saw him that evening, she asked him if he was ill, and, as Sergi said he was fine, she showed him the dirty underpants. 'Does this often happen?' she asked. The boy went a deep red and shut himself in his bedroom.

'Find that shocking?' asked the second cop, who'd been listening to Martínez tell the story while chewing gum mercilessly. 'You just wait, *the* worst is to come.'

'Three days before Christmas Rosa decided to meet the manager of one of the hotels in the chain she worked for as an accountant. He'd been pursuing her for some time. They strolled around the Port Olímpic and he invited her to dinner in an expensive restaurant, where most diners spoke English, German, Swiss, and other languages they couldn't pin down. Then he suggested going for a drink, and on the sea front, opposite a half-empty glass of whisky and Coke, he revealed his intentions by bringing his lips close to hers in a rapid, almost furtive, movement. She let the first kiss go ahead but broke off the second, apologized abjectly and went home.'

'She'd had a premonition,' added the second cop, winking at Jia.

'Will you let *me* finish?' Martínez lifted a hand to shut him up. 'Some things are not a joking matter.'

'Rosa walked into her flat. When she saw a light on in Sergi's bedroom, she quickly entered the bathroom and shut the door behind her: she felt as if she'd done something wrong, and needed a few minutes to think up an alibi. She didn't have to tell any outlandish story. She went into her son's room after calling to him a couple of times and getting no response, and what she found made her faint. Her son was lying there in his underpants with his head blown to pieces, surrounded by a dozen huge cuddly Santa Clauses. The barrel of the gun was still in his mouth, and his hands were gripping the butt. Twenty or so crickets were crawling over his bed; they'd been released from the boxes in which the pet shop sold them: that food for snakes and chameleons had become the funereal accompaniment to a spectacular suicide, news of which spread through the neighbourhood on that dreadful day as quickly as those escaping beasties. In the meantime, Rosa, transformed by her neighbours into *Senyora* Rosa—an attitude of deference that separated them from her—went steadily downhill.'

'It was *the* foulest thing to happen in the Eixample for years,' the second cop declared: his sourpuss face was his attempt at displaying compassion, though his impoverished language meant every one of his comments sounded more like a wisecrack.

'You must be patient with her,' pleaded head cop Martínez, before lighting a last cigarette. 'She'd never hurt anyone. Now it's almost Christmas, her crisis attacks get worse. We'll go to her flat for a moment. I don't suppose anything has happened, but better to be on the safe side.'

Jia ought to have asked about the man who'd taken her away. What was his role in all that? He didn't, because he was so shocked, and when he was alone with Liang, he poured two Cokes laced with whisky and they whispered nervously as they sipped. On the one hand, they'd have preferred not to see that woman ever again. On the other, they were curious to find out more about what had had happened over the last two years of her slow degeneration, now possibly crowned by a potentially self-inflicted injury. There were still traces of blood on the bar floor.

After two hours and a half, during which they gave the bar a thorough clean, the Raj Kapoor film ended and it filled up with film buffs waiting for the next session to start. Brian de Palma's *Phantom of Paradise* had attracted quite a number of university students. Jia and Liang served over thirty Coca-Colas and beers in under ten minutes. Their brisk business made them forget the story of *Senyora* Rosa and her son Sergi. Enthused by the clatter of coins whenever Liang opened and closed the till, Jia again reminded himself he was a lucky man and shut his eyes for a few seconds to savour the pleasure of such a sentiment.

The bar quickly emptied. Their stress returned. Liang said she had no desire to see *It's a Wonderful Life*. Jia felt that was reasonable enough. He was in no mood to see the film either.

'In real life, the day you decide to commit suicide, no angel will ever make you see sense,' he said in Mandarin, recalling the film's basic plot: James Stewart's visitor from the world beyond had invited him to think how important he was to others by taking a walk through various moments in his life.

Jia went out for a breath of fresh air, but rather than standing in front of their bar he started to walk. Initially he seemed quite lost. Then he spotted a drop of blood on the ground and decided he must follow the lady's trail until it petered out. No sooner said than done: he walked two blocks and on the Carrer París turned right. The Escola Industrial was opposite the pavement where he'd been pursuing the drops of blood. He stopped in front of a doorway where more blood had been spilt, and where the boots of head cop Martínez and his colleague must have trod. *Senyora* Rosa lived there. If the door had been open, he'd have gone up to her landing and turned around and gone back to the bar. As it wasn't, he turned tail, ready to walk off, but after taking only a few steps, he instinctively glanced back up at the balconies. Two old ladies were staring down at him and muttering. Jia noticed he was getting goose bumps. He crossed the road, waited a few minutes, not quite sure why, and stared at an attractive, olive-skinned girl walking by, glued to her mobile. He retraced his steps, still half-stunned, and, when he entered his bar, he saw the man with the shiny baldpate and inquisitive eyes by the counter.

'Good evening,' he said, as Jia walked past.

Jia nodded, then immediately looked at Liang who was nervously making the man's cup of coffee.

The man sneezed to catch the couple's attention, something he did without having to overexert himself.

'I do apologize for leaving without paying before. I could do nothing else in those circumstances. That woman . . . *Senyora* Rosa . . . You know who I mean?'

Liang brought him a cup of steaming coffee.

'Here you are,' said the man, giving her a five-euro note. 'Will that cover it? I mean this coffee and the one earlier? I don't like to be in debt to anybody.'

Jia stood in front of the sink and started washing cups and glasses. Lian began cleaning the coffeemaker. In the meantime, the man leafed through a free newspaper and slowly sipped his coffee.

A quarter of an hour passed, two girls came in and ordered tonic waters and Jia and Liang made a couple of trips to the bathroom and storeroom. They exchanged a number of words in Mandarin: she scolded him for going off for no reason at all: he replied, none too convincingly, that he'd gone out because he'd been feeling queasy, but then he confessed he had gone in search of the *mysterious woman's* front door.

'I wanted to find out more,' he told Liang.

She snapped: 'That was a waste of time.'

He could have continued his investigation by asking the stranger something, but they didn't dare. In fact, the man took the initiative, just before he left. He said he'd almost finished a book on his two neighbours, Amèlia and Concepció. They were completely in the dark: it was practically top secret, but one day they'd find a copy in their postbox, in a modern, posh paperback edition. He explained how their snooping behaviour had made his life misery, and one day he had decided he couldn't stand it anymore, and had walked out to his gallery and threatened them with a puerile gesture, transforming his hand into a pistol that rang out: Bang-bang. They reported him. At first, he took it to be a joke. However, a court case had been opened against him and it really hurt: the prosecution was demanding a thirty-thousand euro fine and three years in jail. He'd know what his sentence was by the end of the month.

Rooted to the spot, a deadpan Jia listened to his story, and finally asked: 'So what's *Senyora* Rosa's got to do with all this?'

'I'm afraid she'll be those neighbours' next victim. The writing is on the wall: they're implacable.'

The man jumped off his stool and waved goodbye. That was the last Jia and Liang heard about any of all that. About him or the woman. Or the neighbours. They sublet the bar three weeks later and opened a hairdresser's next door to the Estació del Nord on the other side of town.

Which Country Do You Want?

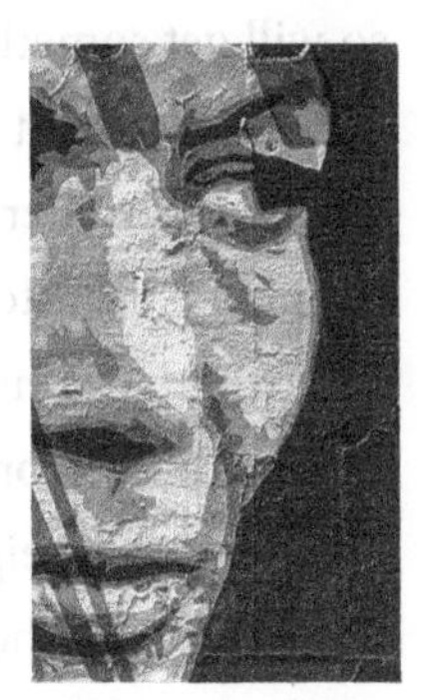

Empar Moliner

'Now then, which of you is Colombian? They want a Colombian who's got papers. It's for a family with two children.' Shouts go up from the room that is crammed full: 'I'm Peruvian, mother!' But Sister Encarna, a slight, energetic nun, knocks on the table: 'Order! I said: "Colombian", can't you listen properly?' And she then adds quietly: 'Work will come, it will, just be patient.' She speaks to a girl carrying a free daily in her denim jacket pocket. 'And it's only your first day here . . .'

The scene—around a hundred Latin American women hoping to be hired as home helps—is repeated every morning in the lobby of the convent of the Immaculada Concepció de Castris in Barcelona's upper reaches. Ten or so will get something. The almost eighty others will ask to be put on the list for another day and go home with a box of biscuits under their arm (a gift from the parish). But people also go to the convent in search of maids. Right there they scrutinize the candidates, set out their priorities (with papers in order or not, experience, age, even country of origin, and weight), make their choices, and, sometimes, take them with them. Sister Encarna is answering the phone all the time: 'So she didn't turn up? You know, I do keep telling them, but they find honesty hard, and, you know, I do insist. You have to realize it's another culture. When the job doesn't interest them, they don't show up and that's that. I'll tell them all this very minute. Yes, thanks be to God that they're not all like that . . . Yes, yes, yes. Everything is fine and dandy, and then they don't turn up. Yes, I'll send you someone else. Good heavens, I'll do that straight away. All right, *senyora*?' She puts the telephone down and squares up to one of her helpers, a young Ecuadorian girl who's eating biscuits like the ones they just handed out. 'It's what I keep telling you. You don't speak straight. We have to behave ourselves.' She gets up and addresses all the women: 'Listen to me, because this is important. Somebody has not turned up at their work-place.' Loud rumblings of disapproval around the room. 'She should have rung, mother,' shouts a girl carrying a baby round her neck. More women put themselves forward ('Mother, you can send me . . .') and the nun knocks on the table again: 'The person to go must know how to run a household and look after a sickly eight year old. They pay six hundred and sixty euros.' This time the rumblings are approving, and a woman, next to me, tells me this is the maximum usually paid for temporary work. Her name's Rosa Trujillo, she's Peruvian, and has lived here for ten years and works nights looking after an old man and mornings house-cleaning, but in her spare time works as a volunteer helper for Sister Encarna. 'The drama', she tells me, 'is that most of these women have been brought up to be submissive and accept male domination. A lady came to ask for help the other day. Her husband brought her and their children and, once he'd settled them in, he went back to Lima with another woman. Many of us come here because an employment agency keeps back part of the money, that's not very much anyway. And another problem is that the people who've just arrived think that if they lie it will make it easier to find work. For example, they *kill off* their husband and children, because they think it's better to say that they are on their own.'

Someone rings the doorbell and the biscuit-eating helper runs to shoo away the women crowding in front of the door. Three people, a young married couple and a beautiful blonde, walk in; they want a housemaid. The helper quickly gets them chairs and shuts the plastic concertina door separating the office from the waiting room. 'Come in, ladies, come in,' says the nun. The beautiful lady smiles: 'Sister, I've so wanted to meet you. I have a Colombian you recommended to me and I'm so happy with her. Now I've brought these friends, who've come from afar away and are expecting a child, and they are *awfully* embarrassed . . .' They both take a look around and smile pitifully. 'Well, there certainly are a lot . . . so many people . . .' she mutters. 'Well, I expect you'd rather not know the ones who never make it off the street . . . ,' exclaims the Sister. And then, the practical sort, she immediately asks how much they are prepared to pay. The husband suggests the figure of six hundred. 'Well, really,' the nun protests, 'if you could push it up a bit . . . Looking after a child as well!' The husband raises it to six hundred and fifty and the Sister shrugs her shoulders: 'Well, that's up to you. You live outside Barcelona and that's what they're paying for a live-in. And two half bonuses. And a month's holiday. What age person do you want?' Their friend interjects, 'Sister, I advised them to go for a girl who is a mother.' The Sister makes a note of that. 'Fine, and what country do you want?' Their friend interjects again. 'You know, as I'm so pleased with Colombia . . .' This time the nun shakes her head: 'We don't get very many from Colombia. And not too old, I suppose?' She opens the sliding door and goes out to look for a likely candidate. 'This is very hard, very stressful,' mutters the pregnant wife. And when the biscuit-eating helper hears that, she exclaims: 'And some have been here five months and still haven't found work.' But now the nun comes back with the woman she has selected, an Ecuadorian, who sits down in front of the three of them for the interview. While she answers questions (whether she has children, her training, . . .) her eyes come to rest on a wooden plaque where the letters in relief say: 'Suffering in silence with a smile on your lips and sorrow in your heart, is a sign of the most exquisite, spiritual elegance.' The conversation is a short one and the candidate is at once dispatched back to the waiting room. They have rejected her because she is looking after her parents-in-law and can't sleep away from home. Someone else knocks on the door. This time a lady wearing a fur coat and black leather gloves comes in. She is a helper and is about to give a talk ('on good behaviour', the nun tells me). She begins by advising all those women not to lie to the Sister, who is doing everything 'for their own good'. Then she explains what rights immigrants have, like the right to social security. At the back of the room, someone retorts that that isn't true. 'It is,' she answers with a smile. 'I went to find out what they are, you didn't. Social security is a human right that you do enjoy here . . .' While the debate goes on, the biscuit-eating helper places her mobile on the window sill to check whether there's coverage.

MAPFRE

The Sound of Keys

Najat El Hachmi

1

My sister and I came to live in Barcelona. We'd often visited the city and been fascinated by the bustling streets, the crowds, the metro doors when they shut, the noise, the shops we entered and exited without anyone saying a word. Everything seemed to give off cheerfulness that was also perhaps ours at being away from the neighbourhood where we'd grown up, which was several blocks of flats built around a small square. We spent summer afternoons in that square. Our small world was on the town outskirts, in the middle of fields that were an undulating green in spring. I'd often while away the time watching the swaying ears of corn from the flat we shared on the seventh floor of our red-brick block.

When it was almost summer and the humid heat clung to our skin, that green changed into a dazzling sea of gold, but the reapers soon arrived. Then the fields became barren wastes and I'd feel a strange lump in my throat. My sister did too. She didn't tell me, but I knew. I'd stand by the window and ask her: don't you think this is a sad time of year? And, stretched out on her bed, she'd not look up from the book she was reading, but would say: sadness is supposed to be autumnal. But she felt the same heaviness on her chest that wouldn't let us breathe. Now and then she too sighed deeply.

We came to the city at the start of summer. *Nena*—my sister called me '*nena*'—it's so hot here. On the whole journey in the train, clinging to our suitcase handles, we kept handing the keys to the flat back and forth, making a clatter that Mother hated. She said it would bring bad luck, quarrels. But we'd left home to see the back of ridiculous rules like those she and Father imposed.

The flat had two rooms with a couple of windows that looked over a narrow yard, though there was some light because it wasn't a very tall building. The deafening din from Meridiana and Carrer Aragó was quite subdued by the time it reached us. And although we didn't have a door out to Pasatge Vintró, inside the flat we could smell the chlorine from the Vintró sports centre.

When we walked into the flat, we left our cases in the entrance and walked around. We threw our arms in the air as if we had rented a mansion. We jumped and laughed and felt a tickle in our tummies and throats. We looked at each other and clasped hands. We spent ages acting foolishly like that, but ours really had been a silent revolution. From then on, we alone would decide what and how we wanted to live.

There was one mattress. Nothing else. For the moment we put it in the space that should have been the dining room. We'd mainly brought clothing with us from home. My sister had also brought books that weighed a ton. I tried to persuade her not to. She said no, nobody at our parents' would read them. We had already started to say 'at our parents'. And it was true: we were seven brothers and sisters, and she was the only one who liked books. Come on, let's go out, I said. Shouldn't we put our clothes away? I persuaded her we could do that later. I was sure that if we opened our cases, we'd start talking about our parents, brothers, and sister, about the only girl whom we'd left behind because she was too young, and we couldn't wait until she came of age. Then we'd feel remorse. All the remorse we'd been feeling since we decided months ago that we had no choice but to leave. We were sick of that square surrounded by blocks of flats, of the boys who chased us down the street and, if we didn't take any notice of them, threatened to spread nasty gossip about us. I didn't know how to keep quiet about my dates with the boys I did like. My sister didn't have that problem. She believed in love, in finding someone she'd understand as if they'd known each other forever, like a missing half, she'd tell me. I told her such a thing didn't exist and the idea probably came from the upbringing we'd had, that it was a way to justify obeying the rule about staying a virgin until you married. She said that wasn't the case, it came from the books she'd read. What a pity, I insisted, you're missing out on such a lot, love comes with practice. But it was to no avail, I never did change her mind.

2

Walks. Walks, nonstop walks along the city's endless streets. Barcelona *was* endless, and that's what we most liked about it. We went down as far as Les Glòries, we crossed over to Poblenou, and from there took any street that led to the sea. Not knowing we would reach the sea. Not knowing a thing. We were like country bumpkins, gawping at everything. We'd been to Barcelona before but only for specific reasons. For years, the whole family had come by train, to sort out our papers. My sister and I found it embarrassing when we all got on the train, we were so many brothers and sisters, so many children. The two youngest still quarrelled and Mother sometimes slapped them. And in the Metro she'd shout, hey, you, be careful, all the time and hold out her arms in front of us so we didn't fall on the tracks. Our mother was a mother-hen. Father was quieter and always chewed something. Whatever did he chew? I don't know why we were so embarrassed. Perhaps because we were such a raggle-taggle, were so many. Because we were different and the rest of the passengers stared at us. Our parents were fat. Father had a paunch but Mother was one huge bulk. Seven pregnancies. One after another. We knew that if we left, we'd not be around to help her, but we couldn't do anything about that. We couldn't continue to cook for nine, prepare the teas Mother often organized at home with other women, clean and tidy the boys' rooms because there was no way we could convince her we girls weren't born with a natural gift for housework, while boys weren't allowed to clean, cook, or pick up their dirty underpants from the floor. Then she complained and shouted at them not to leave everything in a mess, she'd say you'll be the death of me, as she bent over to collect up their dirty clothes.

We'd also come to the city months ago looking for a flat and work. But we always went to specific places. A temporary employment agency, an estate agency. We left our curriculum vitae in the Vila Olímpica, the Ramblas, etc. Always keeping it a secret from Mother. We pretended we were visiting a girlfriend's place and spending the day there and we asked our friend to lie for us. Father worked ten hours a day and never noticed. We just had to make sure we didn't get back late for supper.

I found a job dishwashing in a restaurant in the Vila Olímpica, one of those near the water's edge. Throwing away leftovers, rinsing dishes, putting them in the dishwasher, washing huge saucepans, doing whatever I was ordered by the cook, a tall woman who was always laughing. When I finished, I went to the nearby discos and watched the go-go girls swaying in their platform shoes, miniskirts, or hot pants, their firm flesh in fishnet stockings. I wanted to touch them, but only stared. My sister came once and immediately started to whinge. The music was too loud, the place too dark, it wasn't her thing. But I left her to go to the toilet and when I came back she was staring at a go-go girl, as if she'd been hypnotized. When she saw me, she said, come on, let's leave. And we left to sleep on that dirty mattress under the window. The snoring that came from the yard and the curtain that flapped if there was a breeze made my sister and me feel uneasy. It was a diffuse disquiet, not like the heaviness on our chests. We lay down with our backs to each other and talked in the dark. I never told her, but I don't know what I'd have done if she hadn't come with me and we hadn't shared that dirty mattress. Perhaps we felt uneasy because the flat was empty; we'd still not had time to buy furniture. And we were used to the cramped spaces in those tiny flats, with bunk beds and blankets piled everywhere and loads of cups and dishes on the side in the dining room, the gilt-framed pictures

Father suddenly got a craze for, the carpets we had to clean, the shoes the nine of us stacked by the front door because Mother said only pigs walked inside their home in shoes worn in the street. And then there was the television, which was always switched on. My sister and I now led a silent life, in a space with one mattress and two open suitcases that seemed like a constant throwback to our previous life.

We started making lists the day my sister went to the disco with me. Lists of things that came into our heads before we fell asleep. To appease the silence, but also so as not to be left alone with our thoughts.

3

We went to IKEA and bought nothing. We still didn't know what we wanted our home to be like. And we repeated 'our home'. Our life will be like our home, said my sister. We walked gleefully down the aisles, swept along by the infinite possibilities offered up by that ocean of space. Life's potential, my sister repeated. There was no IKEA in the blocks of flats in our neighbourhood. Our cheap furniture looked cheap. Not like the Swedish store where what was cheap looked expensive. We bought glasses and plates and cleaning stuff. Just for us two, for the moment. I was pushing the cart and my sister suddenly appeared from one of the passageways with a huge casserole. What are we going to do with that?, I asked and she said, lunch or dinner. And didn't she see it was too big for two, that it was more like for nine. And what if they pay us a visit? Do you think all seven will ever come? You can bet Mother will, when she's got over her upset, she'll want to come and see where we live, the rest won't. Father definitely won't. But what if we have guests? I persuaded her to leave the casserole but she didn't say a word on the journey home, and looked bewildered, rocked by the movement of the train. You mean we'll never cook for so many people. And it wasn't a question. That night, after eating rice and tuna, after working out a budget for what we could spend on furniture and leafing through the catalogue, we added to our list before falling asleep:

- Mother's swollen feet when we arrived in the Port of Almería after hours in the car. She took her shoes off, and there was a deep red weal.
- Father in swimming trunks, Mother sitting on a towel under a parasol, her sleeves rolled up, never going near the water's edge. Only that day when we persuaded her and she held our arms tight while dipping her feet in, as if the sea might sweep her away. She could see it wouldn't, because our brothers were swimming and jumping nonstop; she was really frightened.
- The day that Father told us to go and swim behind the rocks. That it wasn't decent for him to see us like that, half-naked. And he said that to Mother, not us.

4

My sister found work cleaning flats and that wrenched us apart a bit. She started early in the morning and I finished very late. As I'd find her asleep in bed, I started to eat something with my work colleagues. The waitresses wore their hair in a ponytail, were straight-backed, and used lots of makeup. The restaurant provided uniforms, as it did for the boys, but the blouses had pleats and clung tight to their breasts. One was a Vanessa, though we called her Vané, she walked on very high heels, balancing a number of dishes on her hand and forearm. She was really quick and remembered everything she had to serve. My uniform comprised loose-fitting dark trousers and a white tunic I had to button up to the neck. One day I went into the lavatories and heard someone being sick. After a while Vané came out and she said that something hadn't gone down well and that things often didn't go down well for her.

I got into the habit of going out with Vané after work. She took me to places I didn't even know existed and then found it hard to remember how we'd got to them. One day we went to a kind of disco or bar with music which they'd furnished with beds rather than tables and chairs. Loads of people were squeezed together on the beds drinking cocktails. Vané invited me to lie next to her and I thought of my sister sleeping alone on the mattress under the window. Hey, come here, said my workmate. When she changed out of her uniform, you could see her arms were covered in tattoos. Thongs were all the fashion then and she wore one that peeped out of her trousers. And her belly button was bare even though it was winter. She only wore her leather jacket when she got on her motorcycle. She had a helmet for me and I rode pillion, put my arms round her waist and my belly and breasts touched her back. She started up the motorcycle and we crossed the city more quickly than I could ever have imagined, my heart thudded so fast I thought it would stop any moment. And not just my heart, my whole body shook as the breeze hit me, as I clung tight to Vané. I thought we would take off at any moment. I wasn't afraid.

5

One day my sister and I quarrelled. She said I should stop going out so much, that I was taking it too far. That lots of nights I got home late and woke her up and she had to get up early and go to work. We decided we should buy furniture and that we should each have our own bedroom. I told her that a workmate, a kitchen assistant, had offered to go to IKEA with us. We went the next Saturday but argued all day because we couldn't agree on the furniture to buy. Whether we should put a sofa-bed in the dining room or just put lots of cushions on the floor to gain space. It was all up to us. In the end we only bought a mattress that we put under the window in the other room. I didn't go out, I wanted to make peace that night and sat on her mattress and asked her what was the matter. No, it's fine, I like it here. You're having a good time and going out with boys but I'm missing something . . . And she couldn't tell me what it was. I bet you've been speaking to Mother, I said, and she said it wasn't that, yes, she had, but it wasn't that. It was cleaning so many hotel rooms so quickly, for a pittance, and the constant din! I can't get used to the din! We both cried for a while and then drew up another list:

- The day those two mothers pulled each other's hair in front of all the children leaving school.
- Yes, those two went crazy and Mother was in the middle trying to separate them. Saying they would bring shame on their families. At least our mother would never do anything like that.
- Our mother's very dignified. When they told her gossip about other girls she'd say everything is in God's hands; she tried to get those who were criticizing to feel sorry for the families of the girls who'd lost their tempers.
- Did she cry when you spoke to her?
- No, she just asked if we were all right, if we needed anything. And I told her we had everything we needed.

We fell asleep, our backs touching, the mattress smelling of plastic. The next day we went to the beach. My sister wore a swimsuit and covered below her waist with her headscarf. She said she didn't like her legs, she didn't want to expose them. I talked to her about having freedom to do whatever you wanted; if somebody didn't like her legs, too bad. But she said it wasn't other people, *she* didn't like them. They were horrible. She said that before Vané arrived, who came to keep us company. When she stretched out on her towel, she undid the top part of her bikini, and told me I'd have marks. I didn't want any marks, but felt stressed about my sister seeing me there in the midst of all those people with my breasts bare. And I muttered to myself, look, all that talk about freedom and it turns out you're the prude. And I said goodbye to modesty and undid my bikini top. My sister wasn't looking at me. I wasn't looking at her. Vané's breasts were very round and when she stretched out, they didn't hang down her sides like mine. She noticed I was staring at her and said 'touch them if you want.' I put my sunglasses on and stretched out again.

6

One day my sister came home on a high. It was Sunday, she had got up early and gone out for a walk. Sunday is the best day in Barcelona, she said. There aren't so many cars and you see things you don't notice on a weekday. There's a centre near here with people like us, very nice, very open people. Young people who come together to do activities, to talk about life and death, etc. One young girl was organizing a bicycle rally! Can you imagine Father or Mother taking part in anything like that?

She talked about that centre nonstop while I got dressed and then we went to have lunch in a nearby restaurant called La Lluna. She didn't say as much, but I guessed it was a religious centre. She told me it had a carpeted room where mothers learned to bring up their children with proper values. *Our* values, she said, and I looked at her speechless; it was as if my sister had suddenly distanced herself from me. We went to the gym in the afternoon. We had become members of the gym on Passeig Marítim, because that way we could go straight to the beach when we left, but that day my sister said she wanted to stay on and do more exercises, that she didn't like sand. I tried to persuade her to go out at night; she'd not done so for ages. You be careful, she said.

We'd agreed to meet Vané and a boyfriend of hers in the bar with the beds, that I now knew was near the Plaça del Pi and, after going to a couple of places in the area, we ended up sprawling there. My head was in a spin, I felt it was really light, as if I'd got rid of a heavy burden I'd been carrying for a while. The beds in that bar were uncomfortable; we piled on top of each other and I didn't know what to do with my legs. I thought it was filthy to put my shoes on the bed. I was in the middle, between Vané and her friend, who smelt of that deodorant adverts say is attractive to all women. Now and then I could feel the skin of their arms rubbing against me on both sides. They were kissing on the mouth right in my face and I stared at them. Then they burst out laughing.

We went to the bathroom and Vané said I should take him home, it was obvious we were both dying for it. And why not his place? I said, worrying about my sister. He can't. He'll tell you why, if he wants to, but you can't go to his place.

He too had a motorcycle. I got on the back and we went to Passatge Vintró. I tried not to make a noise when he was kissing the back of my neck. I thought I was still on the bike and we would take off at any moment. But it wasn't the case, we had to take our shoes off and slip into the bedroom with the new mattress that smelt of plastic. I tried to muffle the moans, mine and his, but it was hopeless. You bet my sister could hear us on the other side of the partition.

7

We fell asleep. I told him he'd have to leave before my sister woke up, but neither of us managed to get up before one. She wasn't in the dining room. He'd left by the time she got back.

'I can't stand it,' she said calmly. 'It's one thing for you to be free and another for you to bring men home. Freedom is one thing, one-night stands are another.' And we argued, I told her it was my home too, where was I supposed to go to have a little privacy? and she said no way, that was a place just for us two, for our new life, and not for endless fucking. And she kept repeating the word 'fucking'. And I couldn't understand why she was so angry. I heard you, she said, I heard you when you arrived. You're just like our father, I retorted, a hypocrite. Must I go behind rocks to do what I feel like doing with my body? And then she started repeating I've had enough, as she stuffed her clothes into her suitcase. This is no place for me.

At that point I could have begged her to stay, said we needed each other's company in the new life we'd just begun, but I didn't. I let her leave after she'd put her shoes on by the front door, and thrown me her set of keys.

24

The Boy Who was Sure to Die

Quim Monzó

He lived on the Diagonal, near Entença, on the sea side of the street. I was ten and he was perhaps eight. He was thin and looked pallid and frail. His father, a doctor, always told his wife: 'Don't you worry, rely on me to find a cure. I promise I will.' And, true enough, he put his energies into it: he spent hours and hours every day looking at entries on his son's illness in medical reference books, and wrote to specialists around the world in an attempt to find a solution.

I was the son of a seamstress and, sometimes, during the school holidays, my mother took me with her so I wasn't left on my own at home. She went to a different lady's house every day. I loved going to these ladies' houses, provided they gave me a pile of magazines to read. We never had any and these ladies my mother sewed for had lots. Magazines crammed with words and black and white photos, even rather faded coloured ones, a result of the technology of the time. Apart from magazines some houses had Coca Cola, which was a luxury product in my eyes. I'd never seen a bottle at home. One day I'd watched the boy from the grocery store bring a cart full of crates of bottles to one of those flats—that belonged to a dentist on the Gran Via. Every afternoon I went, the lady asked me if I'd like a Coca Cola and I always said no. Surprised by my reply, she insisted, but I stuck to my guns, although deep down I was dying to have one.

On Thursdays, my mother always sewed at the house of the lady married to the doctor whose son was ill. They took me to the boy's bedroom and we played. I only ever saw the boy in his bedroom. Never in the dining room or lounge. When I arrived he was in bed in his pyjamas. He was always in his pyjamas. He had lots. Pyjamas with red and white, blue and white stripes, some all blue or grey with white piping. Maybe he was pallid because sunlight never touched him. At half-past four they brought us a snack on a tray with wheels. A snack for both of us. Milk and biscuits. The same for me and him.

I was intrigued by the fact that he never went to school, that he was so sick he could always stay at home, and was spared classes, teachers, schoolmates, and stupid jokes. He was a nice, well-mannered boy unlike the wild animals who ran around the desks at my school. As his health was so delicate I deduced that he would die before making it to be an adult, though nobody said that out loud and the lady always told my mother her husband always said he would move heaven and earth to find a cure: 'I promise I will.' My mother said he never played with other children because he didn't have any brothers, sisters, or cousins, or any friends (he never left the house) or schoolmates (he never went to school). That was why when we reached the magnificent entrance to their house, before ringing the bell, my mother told me to be nice to the boy, poor thing. That 'poor thing' was another sign that he must really be in bad shape.

I played with him and was nice, among other reasons, because I was nice to almost everyone and didn't need to be told to be so. One wall in the boy's bedroom was lined with shelves full of table games and toys, from ceiling to floor and one end to the other. They contained all the games and toys that fascinated me in shop windows, and that I would never own. The one I liked most was a basketball game, a plastic and cardboard pitch about a metre wide with all manner of levers that, if properly activated, when the ball fell into one of the two holes it had, allowed you to score a basket. A coloured drawing of three basketball players chasing the ball was on the lid; it was a lovely box. We often played at that, and not on my say-so; it happened to be one of the games he preferred.

Generally speaking I liked to help myself. When I went to the market with my mother, I always came back with my pockets full: spoons I filched from the crockery and pots and pans stalls that were outside, the odd cup, plastic soldiers and toy rubbish carts, and comics I hid under my jersey. From other houses where I accompanied my mother I lifted glasses with French brand names and engravings, and figurines, and imitation—I imagine—Roman lamps . . . I never lifted anything from the boy's house. And it would have been easy enough. Obviously I could have taken the basketball box or games compendium, or the small billiards table, or lifted balls, packs of cards, or those pinball squares covered in transparent plastic with holes and channels to ping balls along. I could have left with several such toys; he had so many he'd never have noticed. But I never lifted a thing because I knew that someday soon the boy would die, and, given he had no siblings, who would they give some, if not all the toys, to? I didn't discount the possibility it might be me, because I'd kept him company and played with him on all those afternoons my mother took me along when she went to sew.

One winter Thursday when I was at school, my mother went to the house but the lady didn't open the door as usual, her sister did and she told her: 'I don't think my sister's in a state for any sewing today.'

When I finished school and arrived home, rather than finding our flat empty, as was usually the case, my mother was there and she told me the boy had died. I entered a state of alert. It wouldn't be today, because they were too overwhelmed by his death, but soon—next week, or the one after, perhaps—they'd tell my mother they had some toys for me. Perhaps they'd want me to go and fetch them, out of a sense of ritual, and, if that were the case, I'd tell them how sorry I was that the boy had passed away. Though, most likely, I wouldn't need to. Perhaps my mother would come home next Thursday with a bundle of playthings and one would be the basketball game. For sure. It would be that game, the one we'd most played together, and they all knew that we did.

Next Thursday, when I got home after school and saw my mother wasn't there—meaning she was back sewing at that house, as before the boy died—I was so on tenterhooks waiting for her that when she came home, I was standing anxiously in the passage. And it was a shock to see her empty-handed. I knew she would scold me for being selfish so I didn't dare ask if they'd told her what they were thinking of doing with his toys, if they were planning to give any to me, the boy who went to keep him company rather than staying at home or playing football in the street. She told me the boy's parents were very sad, which was reasonable enough, but she didn't mention the toys, which was what mattered to me. I asked her what they would do with the boy's bedroom, if they'd keep it as it was, and she looked at me as if she was upset. For a second I thought she suspected why I was so interested, but her shocked expression immediately faded and she said she hadn't a clue what they'd do with it. As she could see that vague answer didn't go far enough, she added that perhaps they'd keep it just as it was for a while, because that's what parents do when a child dies. I knew what she meant because I'd see that in films: a child dies and the parents keep the bedroom as it was when they died. Although nobody sleeps there anymore, they keep the bed as it was, don't touch anything in the wardrobe, and leave the photos on the walls; they convert the bedroom into a shrine: 'It's exactly the same as when he was here,' they say, because that bedroom is the only way they can cling to the memory of their son. But, in this case, the idea that they might convert the boy's room into a shrine came as a terrible piece of news, because it meant they would leave all the toys and games on those shelves: 'just like they were when he was here'. But what's the point of leaving toys on a dead boy's shelves? I felt increasingly dismayed. Toys are for children to play with, and, if the boy they belonged to, is dead, parents should give them to other children, and, above all, to those who kept their son company when he was alive. If they want, they can keep the empty boxes on the shelves, so they look the same, but toys make no sense in the bedroom of a dead boy who's never going to play with them again.

For a few Thursdays I waited nervously for my mother to come home, I kept hoping the boy's parents would decide it wasn't a good idea to convert his bedroom into a perpetual shrine, that it would be best to forget him once and for all and start life anew and, if they couldn't or didn't want to move flat, they ought at least to re-decorate the rooms, especially their son's, so they weren't always seeing it as it was when he was alive. And, if they didn't come to that reasonable enough conclusion, at the very least they should be aware how mean it was to let all those wonderful toys go to waste. However, the weeks and months went by. I never did discover what they did with the toys but the fact is I *never* crossed their minds. I found that insulting. Wasn't I, as *they* were always saying, the only boy who played with him? I finally decided they were simply nasty people, who had buttered me up when it suited them so I kept their son company, but now I was no longer of use, they'd just forgotten me. If there had been other children, cousins or siblings, I'd have understood them not giving me a single toy, but there weren't, and it was quite obvious they preferred the toys to gather dust on those shelves rather than giving them to me and making me immensely happy, the happiest boy in the world. That was when I concluded that they thoroughly merited the death of their son.

Julio, the Parrot, and the Taxi Driver

Jorge Carrión

Every couple, in the heat of infatuation, spends time together, cohabits and loves, creates a language that only belongs to them. That private language, full of inventions, inflections, semantic fields, and hidden meanings, has only two speakers. It begins to die when they separate. It dies entirely when both find new partners, create new languages, and overcome the mourning that lingers on after every death.

The same occurs whenever we move to a new house, whether or not it's in the same city. We change walls and ceilings, neighbours and shops, distances and metro stops. An urban language dies, but as nothing dies completely, part is reincarnated in the new tongue.

There are millions of countless, dead languages.

But their cells survive in prefixes, suffixes, syllables, etymologies, thanks to which they live on.

We came to that flat on Calle Ausiàs March as two people who had just fallen in love. We left it as a foursome, one still in the mother's womb, and a cat. I put it in its carrier. It had spent the last few hours in the emptied flat: that was its last heartbeat.

I closed the door.

I went down the stairs.

Level with my ribs I could feel Julio's tense body, his anxiety through the canvas, his small tugs on the strap hanging over my shoulder.

I took the card with our names out of the postbox.

In the street I stopped the first taxi that passed by.

'I understand if you're stressed,' said the taxi driver after a brief silence, pointing to the carrier on my knees. 'You get very fond of your pets.'

'His purrs are hard to resist,' I replied, the carrier still on my knees, just to say something.

'But, you know, I can tell he's very well behaved.'

'Well, I'm quite surprised, it's only his third time out of the house, and he really is pretty quiet.'

'I've got a parrot.'

'Oh, really?'

'Yes, Lolo, short for Manolo. I love him a hell of a lot.'

As I saw that he wanted to tell me a story, I forgot my musings about dead languages and encouraged him: 'Oh, really? Have you had it for a long time?'

'It's been a couple of years. Choosing one was quite an experience. There are so many kinds, and, frankly, at so many prices. There are the Amazonians, you know, the typical green parrots that everyone owns. Lorikeets are more colourful, but they don't say very much, and hardly interact. Macaws have spectacular colours, and are highly intelligent and sociable, which is all very well and good, but it means you've always got to be paying them attention, because if you don't, they get depressed, and that's like being dead alive. The *yaco* is even more intelligent, as well as being a typical parrot that memorizes words and so on, it can even tell one colour from another. Mine is an African grey. Can't you tell I'm totally besotted?'

'It must be hard to learn how to handle them . . . I suppose they come with an instruction manual . . .'

'I should say so, I had learn to keep him clean and trim, it's really hard to trim its nails, cut its wings, and clean its beak.'

'You have to cut its wings?'

'You bet. You know how you have to take a dog for a walk every day, well, you have to let a parrot out of its cage every day to play. It's fantastic, because he becomes part of the family. And that's when you play, and you *can* play no end with him. And it's not like a dog or cat, where you can only do two or three things. Your relationship with your parrot is—how can I describe it?—more intellectual. I spent weeks teaching him colours with hoops, now he can arrange them by himself, without repeating a single one, red, green, blue, yellow, pink, and so on. Then, you can also give him toys with his food, so he learns to distinguish different tastes and he sees that if he makes an effort and understands the trick, he'll get a prize. He's like a girlfriend or baby. There's a whole lot of toys you can give him They even sell Converse for parrots, no joking.'

'And what do you do when you take him out of his cage?'

'He flutters around. You stroke him. You play with him. But you have to be very, very careful, you know? If you don't watch out, they'll take a peck, because they are so inquisitive, at a piece of chocolate you've left around, or an avocado, or coffee or an indoor plant that's poisonous to them or something soaked in aerosol or cleaning product you use not knowing it's toxic, and they fall ill, and you can't imagine what that's like!'

'Well no, I can't.'

'They are ill, but they pretend they aren't, that they are fine . . . So you're not worried. They're worth every single euro you pay for them.'

'Oh, really?' I said for the nth time, sensing how nervous Julio was, how upset he was getting.

'Yes, they're so goodhearted they worry about you, pretend they're fine, even though the illness is gradually killing them on the inside. And one day, bang, you wake up and he's dead and you think it was a sudden death when he's been dying for months.'

'Amazing.'

'They really love you, you know. Parrots are monogamous. They're very faithful. That's why I bought mine when he was very young because if they don't have a partner, they fall in love with you and love you for ever. You teach them to speak and that's incredible: they speak your very own language. The investment is worth it. I had to get a loan, just imagine!'

'Until death do us part?'

'Yes, siree, until death do us part. That's why most parrots only survive a few days after their owner dies. Although now they've experimented with anti-depressants, Prozac and such like, with some success, so the parrot gets over its loss and can live a few years more. Because in their natural habitat they don't live beyond forty, but in captivity they can make it to a hundred. I hope Lolo lives for years and then stays with my wife, if I pass away first.'

'Hey, that must be one of the few things that's better when you're in captivity.'

'Just so . . . Not long ago they found Churchill's parrot alive, and he's like a hundred and four years old. That's very unusual, because its owner died like fifty years ago. Her name is Charlie, though she's a female. Charlie's very famous in the world of parrots, you know, in parrot mythology.'

'You don't say?'

'Yes, because she learned lots of swearwords against Hitler and against Nazis in general. But she doesn't talk now, though she does dance and so on, but she doesn't talk anymore. They go dumb with age.'

'Not like taxi drivers . . .'

'No, you must be kidding, it's the opposite with us, the older we get, the more we like to chatter . . . By the way, don't you want to know how much Lolo cost? It's the first time a customer hasn't asked me.'

'Some other day,' I replied as I paid him, because Julio had started moving around, terrified by our move.

Notes on the Authors

Miguel de Cervantes (1547–1616) is the greatest novelist in the Spanish language. His *Don Quixote* is the most translated book after the Bible and the cornerstone of the European novel tradition. When writing it, Cervantes was able to draw on a great variety of experiences. As a young man he lived in Italy and studied Renaissance art. He then joined the Spanish navy and lost his arm in the Battle of Lepanto. In 1575 he was caught by the Ottomans and jailed in Algiers for five years. Subsequently, he worked as a tax collector and was jailed for discrepancies in his accounts. After his release, he lived in Madrid and eked out an impoverished life as a writer.

Narcís Oller (1846–1930) is the creator of the modern novel written in Catalan. A member of the *Renaixença* movement that re-established Catalan as a literary language, he wrote novels that explored the impact of economic development on the Catalan countryside and Barcelona. He was translated into many languages and Zola wrote a prologue to the 1875 French translation of *La papallona*, (The Butterfly). He himself translated Tolstoy, Turgenev, Flaubert, and Goldoni. He wrote his most accomplished novel, *La febre d'or* (Gold Fever, 1890–2), about the 1881 Barcelona stock-market crash, in a successful race to finish before Zola published his novel on a similar theme, *L'Argent*. He didn't want to be accused of plagiarism.

Montserrat Roig (1946–91) was born in the Eixample and lived there for most of her life. She was a committed feminist and one of the intellectuals and artists who staged a protest sit-in at the monastery of Montserrat against the 1970 trial in Burgos of the six Basque activists who were subsequently executed. She said that 'she entered Montserrat as a graduate and left as a writer'. Her major novels are *Ramona, Adéu* (1972), which follows different generations of women in the same family, and *El temps de les cireres* (1977), a fictional account of the children of the Prague Spring and May 1968. She was also a journalist and wrote non-fiction, including an account of Catalans in Nazi concentration camps.

Josep Pla (1897–1981) was born in the rural hamlet of Llofriu near Palafrugell. After finishing his law studies at Barcelona University he worked as a journalist in many key European cities and covered the period of hyperinflation in Germany and the rise of Hitler and Mussolini's march on Rome. After the civil war when it became impossible to write in Catalan, he wrote extensively for the magazine *Destino* and became the journalist most censored by Franco's censorship department. His *Complete Works* run to forty-five volumes of short stories, novels, and political and travel writings that make him both the most important and most controversial Catalan writer of the twentieth century.

C. A. Jordana (1893–1958) trained as an engineer but opted to work in the world of publishing, translating, and promotion of the Catalan language during the Second Republic. He was chair of the Catalan Writers Association, a branch of the socialist UGT trades union. Apart from translating English novels by Hardy, Scott, Stevenson, and Huxley as well as *Tristram Shandy*, Jordana is credited with writing the first Catalan noir and the first Catalan erotic novel. He went into exile to France in 1939 and immediately translated twelve sonnets by Shakespeare. In 1940 he and his family sailed to Santiago de Chile and later he went to Buenos Aires to work as an editor at Editorial Sudamericana. He lived in a working-class neighbourhood in Santiago and wrote a novel in a Catalan flecked with Chilean slang about two young tearaways. In the Argentine capital, he wrote his great, Joycean novel, *El món de Joan Ferrer*.

Juan Marsé (b.1933) was born in Barcelona. His mother died in childbirth and he was adopted by the Marsé family. Aged 14 he started writing in literary and film magazines while working as an apprentice jeweller. He later spent two years as a lab assistant at the Institut Pasteur in Paris where he also translated screenplays. By 1967 he was able to give up working in the jeweller's workshop and devote himself to creating his fictional world of young workers, immigrants, and dreamers from the impoverished areas of the Guinardó and El Carmelo, though some writing fell victim to the Francoist censors and had to be published in Mexico, like his masterpiece *The Fallen*, translated by Helen Lane. Many of his novels have been made into films by leading Spanish directors. A major contemporary novelist, he won the Cervantes Prize in 2008, Spain's most prestigious literary prize.

Miquel Molina (b.1963) was born in Barcelona and writes in Spanish. He is a deputy director of *La Vanguardia*, the city's most longstanding daily newspaper. His first novel, *Una flor de mal* (2014), was inspired by research for a story about why Flaubert wrote that Madame Bovary was like 'the pale woman from Barcelona.' His newspaper story and novel lead to Courbet's painting, *La Dame Espagnole*.

Teresa Solana (b.1962) was born in Barcelona. She studied philosophy and classics at Barcelona University and worked in numerous jobs from checkout till at El Corte Inglés to PA to a party leader at the Catalan Parliament. She was also Director of the Spanish Translator's House in Tarazona. *A Not So Perfect Crime*, the first in her Borja and Eduard crime series, won the 2006 Brigada 21 Prize for best Catalan crime novel. 'A Son-in-Law', a story from her collection *The First Pre-historic Serial Killer and Other Stories* is included in the *Found in Translation* anthology of best translated stories from world literature.

Alfredo Bryce Echenique (b.1939) was born in Lima to an upper-class Anglo-Peruvian family related to the Scottish businessman John Weddle Bryce. He studied law at the University of San Marcos but preferred a literary path in life. Like many of the Latin American boom writers he went to Paris and studied in the Sorbonne in 1964 and taught at French universities. His first novel, *A World for Julius* (1970), soon translated into many languages, told of a young man from a rich Peruvian family who found he had more in common with the servants than his family. From 1985 to 2010 he lived in Spain, alternating between Barcelona and Madrid.

Jordi Nopca (b.1983) is the editor of the Catalan daily newspaper *Ara*. In 2014 he won the Documenta Prize for his collection of stories, *Puja a casa*. In 2016 his children's guide to the painter, *A Sea of Stories: Dalí*, was published.

Empar Moliner (b.1966) left school at nineteen and joined an agit-prop theatre group. After a spell as cabaret and theatre artist, she moved into journalism, writing for the Barcelona edition of the national newspaper, *El País*. She made her name as a storyteller in 2004 with the collection *I love you when I'm drunk*, which was voted book of the year by *La Vanguardia* and *El Periódico* and won the La Lletra d'Or Prize. She has become a regular on Canal 3's morning presentations of current affairs with her caustic, incisive wit, while continuing to write a column for the Catalan daily *L'Avui*.

Najat El Hachmi (b.1979) was born in Beni Sidel in the Rif Valley. She emigrated from Morocco to Catalonia with her mother at the age of eight and was brought up in the town of Vic. She has a degree in Arabic language and literature from Barcelona University. Her first novel, *The Last Patriarch*, won the Ramon Llull Prize in 2008 and the Prix Ulysse for best first novel in France. She has since published two more novels about the experience of migration—*The Foreign Daughter* (2015) and *Mother of Milk and Honey* (2018). A fourth novel, *The Body Hunter* (2011), focuses on a young Catalan woman's experience of love and sexual desire.

Quim Monzó (b.1952) has reported from Vietnam, Cambodia, Northern Ireland, and East Africa and has long written several weekly columns for *La Vanguardia*. He has written many books of short stories including *Guadalajara* and *A Thousand Morons* (turned into a film by Ventura Pons) that are characterized by their irony and stylistic precision and have won numerous prizes; most are set in the city of his birth, Barcelona. Quim has also translated many English language authors including Mary Shelley, Truman Capote, J. D. Salinger, and Ray Bradbury. In 2018 he was awarded the highest Catalan literary award for his life's work: the Premi d'Honor.

Jorge Carrión (b.1976) was born in Tarragona but has mostly lived in Mataró and Barcelona, as well as stints in Buenos Aires, Rosario, and Chicago. He writes regularly for the *New York Times* in Spanish and directs the Creative Writing MA at the Pompeu Fabra University. He has written *Bookshops*, at once in praise of bookshops he has visited throughout the world and a history of bookselling. He has also written a book about emigration to Australia, pursuing what happened to relatives of his who went from Catalonia to work in tobacco harvests in the Antipodes. His latest essay is a literary exploration of the many passageways/arcades in Barcelona: *Los pasajes*.

Further Reading and Viewing

There are several excellent guides to Barcelona published by Lonely Planet, DK Eyewitness, Time Out, and Rough Guides. Here are a few books that examine in depth aspects of the city's history and culture.

Barcelonas, by Manuel Vázquez Montalbán (first published 1990; translated by Andrew Robinson, Verso Books, 1992): the late noir novelist visits the different images (Genet vs Gaudí) and villages that make up the city, its tawdry and glamorous sides, at the height of the 1992 hype.

The Gray Notebook by Josep Pla (first published 1966; translated by Peter Bush, The New York Review of Books, 2014) recounts the author's student life in Barcelona, strolling the streets, attending farcical lectures at the university and conversations about Proust, and writing at the Ateneu, drinking in bars, and paying his father's debts. A masterpiece of autobiographical writing!

Forbidden Territory/Realms of Strife The Memoirs of Juan Goytisolo (first published 1985–6; translated by Peter Bush, Verso, 2003) describes the civil war and life in Barcelona from the perspective of a leading Spanish writer who went into voluntary exile to avoid the pain of self-censorship in his writing and intrusive presence of the dictator in his everyday life. The late Goytisolo's mother was killed in a 1938 bombing raid when out shopping for birthday presents for her children.

Barcelona and Modernity: Picasso, Gaudí, Miró and Dalí by Robert Hughes and others (Yale University Press, 2006) examines the development of modernism in. the city's art and architecture from the 1868 Revolution with profuse illustrations.

Jazz Age Barcelona by Robert A. Davidson (University of Toronto Press, 2009) looks at the exciting music scene in the city in the 1920s and 1930s, the bars of Chinatown (El Raval), and the 1929 International Exhibition and the connections between the avant-garde, class conflict, and journalists.

Homage to Barcelona by Colm Tóibin (Picador, 2010) is a lively account of the city's history from a writer who has lived in the city on and off from 1975 and personally experienced the transition from dictatorship to democracy.

Barcelona: The City That Re-invented Itself by Mike Eaude (Five Leaves Publications, 2008) an incisive and entertaining view of the city by a resident who also includes walking tours through various neighbourhoods.

The Barcelona Reader: Cultural Readings of a City edited by Enric Bou and Jaume Subirana (Liverpool University Press, 2017) is full of essays that look at the city from multiple angles: film, noir, cemeteries, street-names, football, asylum, the family . . .

Forgotten Places: Barcelona and the Spanish Civil War by Nick Lloyd (CreateSpace Independent Publishing Platform, 2015) explores all the key civil war sites and figures including Robert

Capa, George Orwell, the Nazis in Barcelona, and Lluis Companys, the Catalan president Franco had executed.

The Struggle for Catalonia: Rebel Politics in Spain by Raphael Minder (C. Hurst & Co. Publishers, 2017) is a history of the city and Catalonia and the development of the independence movement with dozens of interviews with leading Catalan writers, intellectuals, and politicians.

Barcelona: A Culinary and Cultural History of Catalan Cuisine by H. Rosi Song and Anna Riera (Big City Food Biographies, 2019). Barcelonans have wonderful food markets and eat extremely well; this is the first English history of their cuisine.

Messi: Lessons in Style by Jordi Puntí (first published in 2018; translated by Peter Bush, Short Books, 2018) is a series of witty essays by a leading Catalan writer on the Argentine player who has most helped put Barcelona on the map in the twenty-first century.

Novels set in Barcelona (and translated into English)

The Cathedral of the Sea by Ildefonso Falcones (first published 2006; translated by Nick Caistor from Spanish, Transworld, 2008) is set in fourteenth-century Barcelona when the Inquisition was active, the medieval city was at the height of its powers, Santa Maria del Mar was being built, and anti-Semitism was rife.

Victus: The Fall of Barcelona by Albert Sánchez Piñol (first published 2012; translated by Daniel Hahn and Thomas Bunstead from Spanish, Harper, 2014) is a vivid fictional account of the siege of Barcelona in 1714 from the perspective of the Catalan engineer responsible for strengthening the fortifications of the then walled city. The nuns told the defenders: 'Keep fighting, the angels are on their way.' The angels never came.

Barcelona Shadows by Marc Pastor (first published 2008; translated by Mara Faye Lethem from Catalan, Pushkin Press, 2014) is a gothic tale based on a real story that CSI Pastor found in the police archives of real-life child murders in the Raval in 1917 by a female serial killer.

Private Life by Josep Maria de Sagarra (first published 1932; translated by Mary Ann Newman from Catalan, Archipelago, 2015) is a scathing, scabrous portrait of decadent high society in Barcelona where aristocrats embroiled in a not so *dolce vita* are out for themselves and nobody else, too preoccupied with their egos and fetishes to see what was about to hit them.

Field of Honour by Max Aub (first published 1943; translated by Gerald Martin from Spanish, Verso Books, 2009). In this classic, a young man comes of age in Barcelona as the civil war starts and meets anarchists, communists, and chorus girls as the barricades go up.

Uncertain Glory by Joan Sales (first published 1956; re-written version published 1971; translated by Peter Bush from Catalan, The MacLehose Press, 2014). Sales was Catholic, Catalan, and Republican and his tragicomic novel follows the fortunes of a group of student friends from the optimism of the early days of the Republic to the disillusion of defeat.

In Diamond Square by Mercè Rodoreda (first published in 1962; translated by Peter Bush from Catalan, Virago Modern Classics, 2013) set in the district of Gràcia, and narrated by Natalia now looking back at her life from the early days of the Second Republic to the 1950s. An intense portrait of a woman struggling to maintain her children and her sanity in the dark days of defeat and hunger.

Nada by Carmen Laforet (first published 1945; translated by Edith Grossman from Spanish, Random House, 2007). Andrea, a young woman from a small town, arrives in Barcelona full of hope to study at the university. She stays with her grandmother in a gloomy flat in the Eixample and finds her relatives and the city are less than inviting in the drabness of post-war dictatorship.

The Sound of One Hand Killing by Teresa Solana (first published 2011; translated by Peter Bush from Catalan, The Bitter Lemon Press, 2013). Solana's amateur detectives, Eduard and Borja, end up investigating shady business in a New Age Zen Centre on the posh Upper North Side in the San Gervasi district in another satirical take on contemporary Barcelona.

Films set in Barcelona

Barcelona (Whit Stillman, 1994)

Land and Freedom (Ken Loach, 1995)

Todo Sobre Mi Madre (All About My Mother) (Pedro Almódovar, 1999)

Vicky Cristina Barcelona (Woody Allen, 2008)

Biutiful (Alejandro González Iñarritu, 2010)

Cathedral of the Sea (Netflix TV series, 2017)

Publisher's Acknowledgements

Miguel de Cervantes, 'De lo que sucedió a Don Quijote en la entrada de Barcelona, con otras cosas que tienen más de lo verdadero que de lo discreto' (1615), from *Don Quijote de la Mancha*. Alfaguara, 2017.

Narcís Oller, 'El Transplantat' (1897), from *El croquis del natural*. Cossetánia Edicions, 2007.

Montserrat Roig, 'Breu història sentimental d'una madama Bovary barcelonina nascuda a Gràcia i educada segons els nostres millors principis i tradicions', from *Molta roba i poco sabó*.... Edicions 62, 1979. © The Estate of Monserrat Roig. By arrangement with Casanovas & Lynch Agencia Literaria. Permission to reproduce text from William Faulkner, *As I Lay Dying* (Vintage, Penguin Random House, 2004), granted by W. W. Norton & Company, Inc. for electronic rights. For print rights, excerpt from *As I Lay Dying* by William Faulkner, copyright 1930 and © renewed 1958 by William Faulkner. Used by permission of Random House, an imprint and division of Penguin Random House LLC. All rights reserved. Permission to reproduce text from Mary Ann Newman's translation of Sagarra granted by Mary Ann Newman.

Josep Pla, 'Ramon de Montjuic', from *Coses Vistes*. Ed. Diana, 1925. © 1925, Herederos de Josep Pla. By arrangement with Agencia Literaria Carmen Balcells S. A.

C. A. Jordana, First edition: Edicions de 1984, Barcelona. November, 2008 © of the articles of Meridià magazine: 'Clar de Lluna', 'L'hospital', 'El bar'. Permission granted courtesy of IMC Literary Agency. With the kind permission of the Jordana Estate. Heirs of Cèsar-August Jordana represented by IMC Literary Agency.

Juan Marsé, 'Historia de detectives', from *Teniente Bravo*. Seix Barral, 1987. © 1987 Juan Marsé. By arrangement with Agencia Literaria Carmen Balcells S. A.

Miquel Molina, Tres escalones (unpublished), from Pontas Literary & Film Agency. Permission granted courtesy of the Pontas Literary & Film Agency. With the kind permission of Miquel Molina. By arrangement with Pontas Literary & Film Agency.

Teresa Solana, 'Tiempo muerto', from *Barcelona negra*. Siruela, 2016. With the kind permission of Teresa Solana.

Alfredo Bryce Echenique, 'El limpia y la Locomotora', from *La esposa del Rey de las Curvas*. Anagrama, 2010. © 2008, Alfredo Bryce Echenique. By arrangement with Agencia Literaria Carmen Balcells S. A.

Jordi Nopca, 'Las veïnes', from *Puja a casa, l'altra*. Editorial, 2015. © Jordi Nopca, 2015. By arrangement with Casanovas & Lynch Agencia Literaria.

Empar Moliner, 'De quin país la vols?', from *Busco senyor per amistat i el que sorgeixi*. Quaderns Crema, 2005. © 2005 by Empar Moliner. © 2005 by Quaderns Crema, S.A. (Acantilado), Barcelona, Spain.

Najat El Hachmi, 'Soroll de claus' © 2019 by Najat El Hachmi Buhhu. By arrangement with MB Agencia Literaria SL.

Quim Monzó, 'El nen que s'havia de morir', from *El millor dels mons*. Quaderns Crema, 2001. © 1993, 1999 by Quim Monzó. © 1993, 1999 by Quaderns Crema, S.A. (Acantilado), Barcelona, Spain.

Jorge Carrión, 'Julio, el loro y el taxista', from *Pasajes de Barcelona*. Galaxia Gutenburg, 2017, 303-306. By arrangement with Literarische Agentur Mertin Inh. Nicole Witt e. K., Frankfurt am Main, Germany.

Every attempt has been made to contact copyright holders for permission to publish. Anyone wishing to assert their rights with regard to the contents of this anthology should contact OUP.

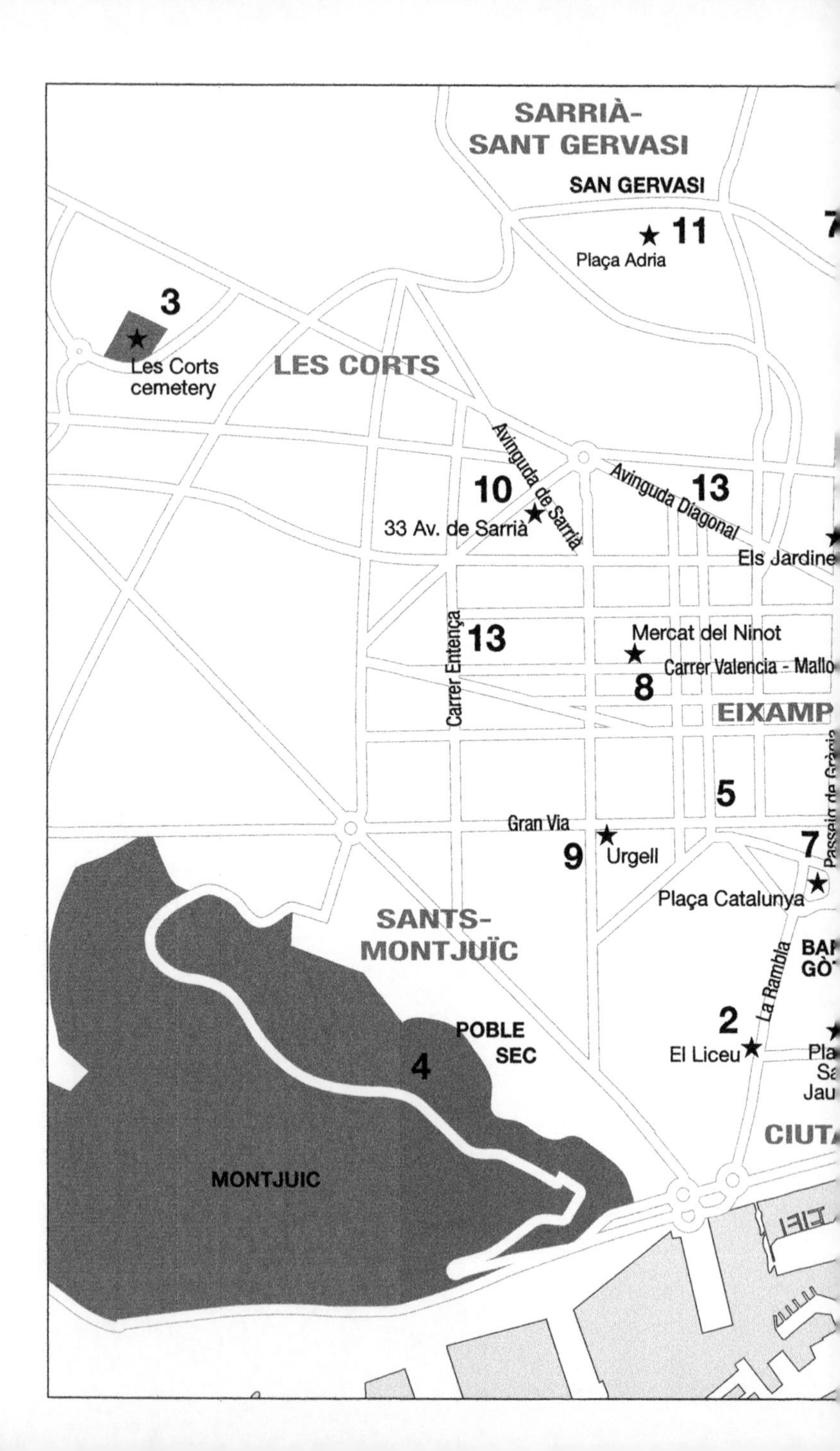
SARRIÀ-
SANT GERVASI
SAN GERVASI
11
Plaça Adria
3
Les Corts
cemetery
LES CORTS
Avinguda de Sarrià
10
33 Av. de Sarrià
Avinguda Diagonal
13
Els Jardine
13
Carrer Entença
Mercat del Ninot
Carrer Valencia - Mallo
8
EIXAMP
5
Gran Via
9
Urgell
7
Plaça Catalunya
SANTS-
MONTJUÏC
La Rambla
2
El Liceu
POBLE
SEC
4
CIUT
MONTJUIC

EL CARMELO
6
HORTA-GUINARDÓ
6
SALUD
ÀCIA
ÀCIA
N
SANT-
ANDREU
SANT
MARTI
12
Gran Via
Plaça
Las Glòrias
14
Carrer
d'Ausiàs Marc
aça
quinaona
Rambla de Poble Nou
Avinguda Diagonal
5
POBLE NOU
ELLA
12
El Port Olímpic